> ## "You are a woman who deserves to be wooed."

How could Briana harden her heart against a man who backed up his words with actions? Flowers, cards with poetry, exotic fruit...?

She waved her hand in dismissal and tried to suppress the jolt of longing his mere presence inspired. "Please, Joseph—"

"Marry me."

"I can't."

"Then tell me why."

"Because... Just because."

"Would it be so difficult to give me the opportunity to change your mind."

"Even if I wanted to let you change my mind, *I can't*." Nerves and sick dread swamped her. Why couldn't she remember what she'd done? Who she'd done it with? "It just won't work."

He tipped her chin up, held her in place with just that gentle touch. "Why do you deny me when you and I know there's something between us?"

Briana felt her emotions teeter over that fine line that held madness at bay, felt reckless words rush forward before she could call them back.

"Yes, there's something there! A baby! And I don't know who's the father!"

Dear Reader,

Every one of us knows that there's that special guy out there meant just for us. The kind of guy who's every woman's fantasy—but only one woman's dream come true. That's the kind of men you'll meet in our new "The Ultimate..." miniseries.

Whether he's the man that'll follow you to the ends of the earth, or the type to stay right in your backyard and promise you a passel of babies, or the guy who'll pull out all the stops in his seduction, the men you're about to meet are truly special.

Mindy Neff kicks off the miniseries. Mindy has always been a hopeless romantic but there wasn't much of an outlet for that as vice president of a construction firm. She'd been reading Harlequin novels for ten years, when her husband urged her to try writing a romance. Mindy loves hearing from her readers; you can write her at P.O. Box 2704-262, Huntington Beach, CA 92647.

We hope you enjoy all the wonderful stories and fabulous men coming to you in "The Ultimate..." series.

Regards,

Debra Matteucci
Senior Editor & Editorial Coordinator
Harlequin
300 E. 42nd St.
New York, NY 10017

# They're ~~She's~~ the One!

## MINDY NEFF

# Harlequin Books

TORONTO • NEW YORK • LONDON
AMSTERDAM • PARIS • SYDNEY • HAMBURG
STOCKHOLM • ATHENS • TOKYO • MILAN
MADRID • WARSAW • BUDAPEST • AUCKLAND

For Lin and Kathy Barry,

Because family isn't only blood, it's deep and abiding friendship. You are truly the sisters of my heart.

ISBN 0-373-16711-3

~~SHE'S~~ THEY'RE THE ONE!

# Chapter One

Nausea churned in Briana Duvaulle's stomach as her gold evening sandals sank into the sinfully rich carpet of the Loew's Monte Carlo ballroom. Her nerves were stretched to the breaking point as she imagined that everyone in the room knew her secret.

Would intermingling with people spark her memory, as Crystal had suggested? Just one day, she thought. One single day that her mind refused to recall. A memory blip that had turned her life upside down.

She hesitated, tempted to turn and run, then checked the impulse and gathered her courage. She'd never been a wimp and had little patience with the turmoil that refused to let go.

Taking a deep breath, she pressed a hand to her stomach. The Principality of Monaco was a little world of dreams. The sea, the rocks, the ancient narrow streets, the gardens that knew no seasons, full of flowers and sweet, heady perfume. All of it should have made the realm an oasis of serenity where love and contentment thrived.

But the Riviera getaway had recently turned into a waking nightmare for Briana.

She was seriously afraid she was losing her mind—a horrible thing for a woman of twenty-six.

She shouldn't have let Crystal talk her into attending this charity function—a fairy-tale ball in a room that sparkled like the Royal Palace—but her cousin's allergies had flared at the last minute and she'd insisted the invitation not be wasted.

Briana's hand trembled against the borrowed sequined bag as she slipped her wrap from her shoulders and moved toward the coat check.

A man stood there, his back to her, his shoulders broad beneath the jet-black tuxedo jacket, an overcoat draped over his arm. She stepped up beside him, and in her nervousness, the evening bag slipped from her fingers.

They bent at the same time. Fingers touched and shoulders brushed as they both reached for the bag. Off-balance, Briana tipped forward. Simultaneously their heads turned…and his lips glanced off hers.

A simple accidental brushing of lips that set off sparks electric enough to rival a dazzling display of fireworks against the French Riviera skyline.

Briana nearly toppled over in her haste to jerk away. The man—who stared back at her with a similar look of spellbound astonishment—simply took her breath away. She tasted the scent of his cologne on her lips.

For what seemed an eon, he stared, as if he could see right into her soul.

Surely he didn't suspect…?

No, no one knew her secret. For tonight, she was

someone else; she could forget—forget the choices that would have to be faced. Still, the way he looked at her, she imagined he could *see* what she so desperately wanted to hide.

And then he smiled—a smile so brilliant, she felt the chaos of her real life slip away, felt her insides turn molten.

He glanced down at the silver-embossed invitation she still held clutched in her hand.

"Crystal Duvaulle?"

She almost didn't answer; in fact had an urge to glance around for her cousin. Then she remembered. The switch. Crystal's allergy attack. The reason *she* was here instead of her cousin. *Mingle,* Crystal had said. *Maybe something will come back to you.*

Briana cleared her throat and stood up. She held out her hand. "And you are?"

"Joseph Castillo. And a handshake seems so tame after that auspicious meeting." His softly accented voice held her entranced, as did his actions. His palm slid against hers, slowly, so sensually she nearly melted. Instead of the traditional formality she'd expected, he drew her hand to his lips and gently brushed a kiss to her knuckles, his gaze holding hers as gently—as surely—as the mere tips of his fingers. Prickles of warmth arrowed up her arm straight to her heart.

Briana felt the blush start at the roots of her red hair and cursed her telling complexion. Crystal wouldn't have blushed; she would have flirted.

And that was when Briana realized that she could, too. She wasn't herself tonight; she was somebody else. What would the harm be?

Steadier now, Briana felt her smile blossom. "I'm charmed. It's been awhile since a gallant gentleman kissed my hand."

"Likewise, Miss Duvaulle."

Laughter tickled her insides. "Gallant gentlemen kiss your hand, too?"

Amusement twinkled in his velvety brown eyes. "Would it surprise you if I said yes?"

She bit her bottom lip. "Maybe. You strike me as being very proper, yet I'd have pegged you as being, uh...straight."

His brows shot upward. "And you'd be absolutely correct. Allow me to clarify. I meant that I, too, am charmed." His dark gaze touched her like a caress, held her, his voice a mere whisper. "More than you know."

Briana's knees threatened to buckle. The power of his sensuality wrapped her in a cloak of excitement. Before she made a total fool of herself, she turned and handed her wrap to the waiting attendant and accepted the claim check. A single look from Joseph Castillo had made her feel as if she were halfway to heaven, sent there on wings of an emotion she'd never felt before.

Moderation was in order, she decided. A little distance to gather her wits. For with his hint of a Spanish accent and his spellbinding gaze, she had an idea she could easily be swept away by this man.

And one foolish mistake in a lifetime was enough. Even if she couldn't remember committing that foolish mistake.

While he was engaged in checking his own overcoat—a necessity due to the gentle rain falling outside—Briana slipped away.

She made several attempts at conversation with other guests, sipped expensive champagne and drank in the opulence of the ballroom. Still, her gaze strayed to Joseph Castillo. And each time she looked his way, he was looking back.

The room was filled with attractive men—dignitaries and a couple of recognizable TV stars—but this man in particular stood out. There was an air of strength and a touch of arrogance about him. His chocolate eyes were faintly bored; his mouth, full and sensual, curved in the barest hint of a smile.

He wore his tux as if he'd been born in one—casually, with an ease that bespoke power and confidence. He had presence, she realized. Although he stood off to the side, he naturally commanded respect and awe. She noted several women dressed to the nines make overtures to get his attention, yet with an almost-imperceptible shake of his head he discouraged the socialites.

Odd, Briana thought. It was as though there was some sort of protocol surrounding this man—a protocol that everybody knew about but her—making it a social blunder to approach him without invitation. People seemed to treat him just a little differently, with deference, she thought, yet he hardly noticed.

Then again, how could he? Briana wondered. He appeared to have eyes only for her. She glanced away, but the power was stronger than she could resist. Like a magnet, his eyes captured hers once more.

He seemed to understand how impossible it was for her to keep from looking. His slow, sexy smile slammed into her like the force of a Grand Prix race car.

His carriage was erect, his stride sure as he crossed the room. And Briana was rooted to the spot, helpless to do little more than stand there and wait for her destiny.

*Coup de foudre,* she thought. Love at first sight. Oh, dear heaven, why now? It was the worst possible time in her life to be blinded by such a silly notion.

But like a sheep without a will, she stood where she was. Watched him. Waited for him. Felt her heart pump and her mouth go dry.

Fine crystal tinkled as glasses were raised and lowered. The orchestra played softly in the background—a waltz, she noted with the small part of her brain that still functioned.

He stopped in front of her, the smell of his cologne surrounding her. She licked her lips; imagined that she could still taste him there.

"It appears we cannot avoid one another," he said softly, his fingertips brushing the tendrils of hair that had escaped her French twist. "Dance with me?"

This is the way a man should touch a woman, Briana thought, dazed, as the pads of his fingers gently caressed her neck and toyed with her hair. He watched her, waiting for permission, an answer to his question. For the life of her, she couldn't remember what that question was. It was as if he were every one of her fantasies rolled into one incredibly virile package, as if she'd known him all her life, when in actuality they'd only exchanged a few words and a few more heady looks.

Then a new thought struck her, one that threatened

her sanity like a splash of ice water in the face, sobering and shocking.

"Have we met before?" she asked, her voice sounding faint even to her own ears.

He grinned and Briana shook her head.

"Believe me," she clarified. "That wasn't a line." One day, she thought. One day that was thoroughly wiped from her memory bank. She had no idea whom she'd met that day or what she'd done. Well, perhaps she had an idea what she'd done, but it didn't bear thinking about.

The madness battered at her again, threatening to bring her down. Turmoil built like a scream. She searched Joseph Castillo's features, praying, yet not even sure what she was praying for.

His smile was gentle, his voice soft. "I would remember if we'd met before."

"One would hope," she muttered.

"One would know," he returned and slipped his hand around her waist, holding his left palm up in the time-honored dance position. "May I?"

She allowed him to draw her close, felt the warmth of his palm seep into her, both calming and thrilling. "We're not on the dance floor."

"We have a floor beneath our feet and music surrounding us."

"Literal, aren't you?"

He smiled and moved her smoothly into the waltz. Guests parted for them as he guided her toward the center of the room. He smelled like heaven and Briana's heart sped up—which had little to do with the exertion of the dance and very much to do with the man who held her so tenderly in his arms.

She felt as though they were the only couple in the room—like in a Cinderella fairy tale. Her world narrowed to encompass just the two of them, thighs brushing, feet gliding with graceful sensuality.

And all the while, his gaze never left her face. It was as if he were determined to memorize every line, every nuance. Likewise, Briana was drawn to him. His sweet breath fanned her cheek, his mouth was so close....

She'd never wanted to kiss a man so badly in her life. Without permission, without invitation. Just to reach up and press her lips to his, taste him, to see if the wild zing pummeling through her system could become any stronger.

*Watch out,* she told herself, closing her fingers into a fist against the fabric of his tux, resisting the urge to test the texture of his hair at the nape of his neck.

*"Una diosa,"* he whispered, his lips curving slightly.

And with that, Briana gave herself a reality check. She chuckled. "I'm hardly a goddess."

His dark brows rose. "You speak Spanish?"

"Mmm. And French and German. Enough Japanese to get me by. I majored in languages."

"Where?"

"Ohio State." She grinned. "You look surprised."

"I wondered. Duvaulle is decidedly French, yet your accent is predominantly American." He dipped her into a turn and Briana followed as though they'd been dancing together for years.

"Deceiving, isn't it. The name's been handed down since my great-great-grandfather. He married an American and since then, the family lineage has become somewhat watered-down. And yours? Castillo is definitely Spanish and you have the accent to go with it.''

"I am afraid my lineage is impeccable.''

"You make that sound like a curse.''

"Sometimes I think it is.''

She wondered at the flash of discontent she saw in his eyes, but told herself it was none of her business. This was just a dance, just one night with an attractive man whom she didn't intend to see again. There were too many uncertainties in her life at the moment and she wasn't about to drag an innocent man into the chaos. No matter how compelling she found him. No matter how right his touch felt.

"So, are you here on holiday?" he asked.

"Yes and no. A working holiday, you could say. And you?''

"Definitely a holiday. I'm looking for someone…a woman.''

Briana felt a swift jolt of pain she had no business feeling. "Have you found her?" Might as well stick the knife all the way in.

"I think I have.''

"Then what the heck are you doing dancing with me?''

"Who's to say *you* are not that woman?''

Briana laughed. Oh, she'd missed this. The thrill and ease of interacting with a man. The engaging of two minds, the ability to pretend for a while that real life didn't exist. "Get real.''

Joseph nearly missed a step in the waltz. Her laughter was full and unrestrained, yet oh-so-feminine. It invited participation. More than one guest looked in their direction, their lips drawn into a smile.

She was an intriguing package. Fairly tall for a woman, yet he liked it. She fit in his arms as if heaven had designed her specifically for him. She had a wholesome complexion like the blush of a new peach, a face that could belong to the girl next door or grace the cover of a magazine. Sexy tendrils of autumn-colored hair escaped a comb studded with rhinestones and fell softly around her neck. Teardrop pearls set in gold hung from the pierced lobes of her ears.

She should wear emeralds, he thought, set in platinum. Brilliant green stones to match her expressive eyes.

She had a mouth that fired his fantasies, lips that appeared to smile often, their natural rose shade subtly accented with gloss.

What intrigued him most of all was that she treated him like a normal man. He couldn't remember anyone ever telling him to "get real." No one would have dared. Nor would they have laughed at his compliment.

"You find the idea of a relationship between the two of us amusing?"

What Briana found was that she couldn't quite meet his eyes. "We've just met."

"Ah, but when in France..." He paused, a dimple appearing in his smooth-shaven cheek. "There is a French expression—*coup de foudre*."

For some ridiculous reason, Briana felt her throat snap closed. There was no way he could have known that was her exact thought just minutes ago. And if her voice actually cooperated, she wasn't about to address that statement. "I'm impressed. Your accent is right on."

"I, too, studied language."

Thank goodness he'd let the subject go. "At Oxford?"

"Harvard. And you did not respond to my excellent French expression."

So, she wasn't off the hook. She hoped she wasn't as transparent as she felt. "No, I didn't."

"Ah, *querida,* I do believe you hold the power to wound me."

"I doubt that. You look like a pretty self-assured guy to me."

"At the moment that is debatable. So, we will come back to this attraction thing later, I think. Tell me of your family."

"Just your everyday family. Dad's a professor, Mom's a nurse. Two sisters and a brother still at home. I'm the oldest."

"And your dreams? What are they?"

*In a mess right now.* "I'd always dreamed of travel. My dad and I used to pour over travel brochures of exotic countries and places. He was never free to do the wanderlust thing because of us kids, but he encouraged me to go for it. So after college I headed for Paris to try my hand at modeling."

"Let me guess. You were on the cheer squad in school, perhaps the drama club, and some smart talent scout discovered you."

"You get two out of three. There wasn't a talent scout. I went in search of that myself."

"And why are you not still in Paris strutting down runways and wearing scary fashions?"

Briana laughed. "Scary is right. Some of those get-ups are really far-out." Her bare shoulders lifted in a shrug. "Competition's tough in Paris. You either have the look or you don't. I didn't, and I'm particularly fond of eating, so I gave it up."

"And came to Monte Carlo?"

"Mmm," she hedged, realizing she was on shaky ground, here. He still thought of her as Crystal. And for some reason she didn't want to correct that misconception. "I have a cousin who lives close by. She invited me to stay, so I came on over."

"An adventurous woman."

"Sometimes more than I should be." Especially that one day. The day she still couldn't recall. Good heavens, just how adventurous she'd been didn't bear thinking about! "So, what are you doing in Monte Carlo?" She paused and grinned. "Or is this starting to sound a little like the Spanish Inquisition?"

He returned the smile. "No. I find it refreshing. The getting-to-know-you process. And I very much want to get to know you."

Briana nearly fanned herself in response to his heated look. A woman could spend a lifetime just listening to that smooth Spanish accent. "You're such a flirt. What do you do, Joseph Castillo?"

The hesitation was only slight. "I'm a businessman of sorts. An ambassador of goodwill for my country."

She grinned, enjoying a little flirting herself. "Is there ill will you're trying to repair?"

"No." His brow arched, his eyes were amused. "We are a peaceful lot. But charity functions such as this and public-relations opportunities are part of my duties."

"Which I imagine means a great deal of travel."

"You sound as if that is a bad thing."

"No. Just my envy showing."

"You'd be surprised how mundane forced travel can become."

"Oh, I'd imagine it'd be pretty tough...what, flying around in a LearJet?"

"Guilty as charged. Occasionally I take the yacht."

"My heart goes out to you," she teased. "You lead a rough life."

"You are making fun."

"Yes."

His thumb stroked her cheek, her smiling mouth. "Your smile is *muy bella*."

"Flatterer."

"An honest compliment."

"Thank you." She knew very well she wasn't a spectacular beauty. Her figure was too well rounded, her feet were the size of small boats, and her eyes were too wide-set. She did have good teeth and a nice smile, though. "Sort of pretty" would be her best description. Still, his compliments made her feel special. And tonight she needed to feel special. Needed a break from the turmoil she would once again face in the morning.

"Tell me about your travels, the places you've been."

And he did. He described the snow in Switzerland so vividly she could almost feel the frigid bite of the wind against her cheeks. He told her of the verdant hills of Ireland, the lush peacefulness of an Amazon rain forest, the smog-filled basins of Los Angeles, the white-sand beaches of Cabo San Lucas, the operas and ballets on several continents.

His subtly accented voice was smooth and rich, quiet and sensual. It drew her in, held her in a spell. His descriptions made her ache with wanderlust.

Time sped past in a haze of laughter and gentle touches, heated gazes and silent speculation. They moved onto the terrace where the lights of the Riviera twinkled like magical diamonds, enchanting, reflecting off the yacht-filled harbor, and stretching along the terraced hillsides and Maritime Alps.

She shivered in the brisk evening air and Joseph removed his tuxedo jacket, draping it around her shoulders, the heat of his body now warming hers.

"Better?" he asked, his knuckles brushing skin bared by her strapless gown.

She smiled. "Thanks. It's beautiful out here, isn't it?" Her voice was hushed, as though to speak louder might disturb the enchantment.

"Yes. Unique and elegant."

She glanced at him, noticing that he looked at her instead of the view. The power of his gaze was almost blinding. Briana cleared her throat.

"Are you one of those lucky ducks with a yacht moored out in the harbor?"

"Mmm." His scent surrounded her as he eased closer, his arm stretching past her. "See the one there?"

"Which one?"

He leaned closer, so that they were cheek to cheek. "Follow the path of my finger. See? The one with the white lights strung from the mast. Just to the right, toward the tip of Nice."

Her eyes widened. "You're kidding. That's not a yacht. It's a cruise ship!"

He chuckled. "Would you like to go on a cruise with me?"

She turned to him, wondering if she sounded as gauche as she felt. This man was out of her realm. She was no American debutante used to living the high life. She'd dabbled in an array of jobs to support herself, from driving a limo to modeling in Paris. Her family was working-middle-class. Like it or not, Joseph Castillo simply awed her.

She expected to see teasing in his eyes. But his dark gaze telegraphed something entirely different. Intense and serious, he watched her, and she realized his offer was genuine. He wasn't toying with her. He truly wanted to see her again.

He made her feel like a princess. She saw his gaze drop to her mouth, knew he meant to kiss her. He slid his thumb beneath her chin, his dark eyes smoldering with need. A need that matched her own.

"May I?" he whispered.

She licked her lips and must have nodded. His hands framed her face. Slowly, gently, he lowered his mouth to hers.

The thrill that shot through her was powerful and drugging. Her hands crept up his shirtfront, rested against his collar, touched the hair at the nape of his neck. Everything seemed to register at once—his taste, his scent, his soft touch that held her more surely than any bonds.

He moved very gently, reverently, the tip of his tongue skimming across the seam of her lips, nipping, teasing, yet never really asking for entrance. It was as if he were afraid to cross some boundary of respect, content to just enjoy, to savor.

She'd never felt so cherished in her life.

*Coup de foudre* echoed in her mind once more, startling her. This man could easily become an obsession. She drew back, touched the corner of his sensual mouth with a single finger, felt her heart twist.

She couldn't have fallen in love so quickly. It was a ridiculous notion. Yet everything within her told her it was so.

And the power of it scared her to death.

She caught the glint of silver at his wrist and read the illuminated dial of his expensive watch.

"Oh, my, look at the time." Her breath heaved in and out as though she'd just run a marathon.

So caught up in Joseph's eyes and voice, Briana had lost track of the evening. She'd never felt so comfortable in a man's presence. She felt as if she knew him, body and soul; as if he were her missing half.

But time had a way of catching up. And her coach was about to turn into a pumpkin. Reality washed over her like the shock of a sucker punch—reality that she'd been able to forget for a few blissful hours.

But now it was back. And she needed to get away. Run before she got in any deeper.

This was a night made of dreams. A man made of her dreams. But he didn't belong to her. She couldn't allow herself to get caught up in the feelings. The hope. Could never—especially now—entertain the idea of love at first sight.

She slipped from his arms and thrust the tuxedo jacket at him. "I've got to go."

She didn't wait for the protest she saw in his eyes,

knew was on the tip of his tongue. She simply turned and hurried back through the emptying ballroom as if the hounds of hell were at her heels.

She had to get out of here. Run before she lost her head completely and succumbed to the temptation—to the fire and longing she saw in Joseph Castillo's handsome gaze. A temptation and fire that matched her own, yet was hopeless.

Hopeless because Briana Duvaulle, perfect little Catholic girl from Ohio, was pregnant and had no memory of doing the deed.

## Chapter Two

Joseph couldn't let her go. He didn't know what he expected from the evening, but he wasn't ready to let it end. He'd been astonished by the blinding attraction he'd felt when he'd first laid eyes on her. His only intention when he'd accepted Jean-Claude's invitation to the benefit was to have a pleasant night out, away from duty and overattentive servants, away from having his every move watched.

Away from the expectations of an entire country.

Now, in the span of one night in Monte Carlo with a mystery woman, he'd felt his life change. He'd felt the shift of emotion, the stimulation of conversation, of flirting, of dancing close and feeling the warmth of a woman's body next to his heart. He felt alive in a way he hadn't felt in years and he didn't want the evening to end. Didn't want the feeling to end.

But his fantasy lady had become edgy. There were secrets in her emerald eyes—secrets he longed to uncover, layer by layer.

He watched the shimmering black of her dress as she hurried toward the door, and he experienced a flash of déjà vu.

In this principality where Princess Grace was legendary, he couldn't help but feel that something special had occurred this night.

Without a doubt, Joseph knew that he had met the woman he wanted to spend the rest of his life with.

*She's the one.*

And she was about to slip through his fingers. He knew her name, knew her dreams—some of them, anyway. But he didn't know her phone number or address. He didn't know her body and soul as he longed to.

He couldn't remember ever feeling this enchanted, as if he were standing on the edge of something wonderful, something life altering.

He caught up with her, surprised her with a gentle hand on her bare arm.

"What is it, *querida?* Why do you run?"

She shook her head and sighed, then stood still, staring at the marbled walls of the elevator. "It's better this way, Joseph."

"Why?"

"Because. There are things about me...." Her voice trailed off. "It's just better."

"It doesn't matter."

"How do you know? You have no idea—"

"It is not important. It is only important that you stay. Please."

She turned, searched his features in silence. A battle waged clearly in her green eyes. He took her hand in his, kissed her palm. He'd never had to beg for anything in his life. He would do it now in a heartbeat.

Strange that he felt this strongly after only one evening. But he was helpless to give it up. To give her up. He wanted to see her smile, listen to her voice, share her dreams, hear her unrestrained laughter.

He needed more time—time to see if he could make her fall in love with him.

"Stay with me."

She wanted to say no; he saw it in the way her auburn brows drew together, in the subtle shake of her head.

"Please? I promise I will not take you anywhere you do not want to go."

"Why do I get the feeling you're not talking about travel?"

His fingers tightened against hers. "There's fire between us. I'm afraid if I let you go, I'll never see you again. It may sound like a line to you, but if that happens, I'm not sure my heart will recover."

She started to shake her head again. He stopped her with a soft kiss on her forehead.

"I've never felt so unsure, *bella*. As if I'm about to grasp something—something important—yet it is threatening to turn to smoke. Help me. Stay with me. Share your dreams with me and I'll share mine with you."

"It's so soon. So fast." Briana brushed a stray curl from her face. She was so tired of racking her brain to explain the unexplainable. She felt as though she were going insane.

How could she be pregnant with no memory of getting that way? One day when a reaction to an antihistamine had created a void in her recall, and now this. To meet a man so attentive, a man with whom, against all reason, she was half in love. The timing was absolutely rotten.

Why couldn't she have met him three months ago?

He treated her like fine china, as if she were fragile, when in fact she was quite sturdy.

He simply swept her away.

What would the harm be? she wondered. To continue the magical evening with this magical man. Why not let fate chart its course? At least this memory would be one she could hold in her heart, a memory that nothing could wipe away.

She glanced at the marble elevator doors, felt her heart pound and her hands tremble, knew what her decision would be. What it *had* to be. What she needed it to be more than she needed her next breath of air.

"Are you staying here? At the hotel?" she whispered.

"Yes. The penthouse suite."

She suffered a moment of doubt.

"I know what you're thinking. Typical playboy lair."

"No. No, the thought never crossed my mind."

He smiled gently at her lie. "I am used to five-star accommodations. Will you come up with me, spend some time?"

She tried for flippancy. "Sure. I've always wanted to get a look at the penthouse."

His fingertip barely grazed her cheek, then swept a path of fire along her bottom lip. "Just be yourself. Relax."

So, he'd seen through her facade. The elevator doors swished closed. She wanted to just look at him for a lifetime. Yet she felt shy. Unable to hold his sensual gaze, she looked away and found their image glancing back at her from all four walls.

Her heart pumped harder. Her knees turned watery as they stepped out of the elevator and entered the elegant suite.

Briana moved to the wall of windows that looked out over the Riviera. Thousands of fairy-tale lights twinkled back at her. She was suddenly so nervous. She'd never gone home with a man on the first date. Never felt so strongly that something was so right. Deep in her bones, she felt the rightness.

Even if she couldn't allow it to last.

But for tonight. Just for tonight, she would accept the journey, live the dream. Tomorrow would be soon enough to face the choices that must be faced.

She saw his reflection in the glass and turned.

Joseph plucked a rose from the crystal vase on the table, held it out to her, remembered a similar act just days ago, in a different room, with a different woman—the *wrong* woman—whom everybody had expected him to marry.

"Roses and emeralds," he said. "You should wear both."

When she buried her face in the fragrant bud, the final combination clicked inside Joseph, fell into place as easily as a key in a well-oiled lock. Perfection. He couldn't say why the action touched him, but it did—in a profound way that he didn't even question.

"Ah, *querida*. You have my heart, I think."

She smiled, pressed her lips softly to the velvet petals. "Do I?"

His fingers touched her hair, reached for the comb

that held it off her neck, released it into a waterfall of soft curls. "Yes."

"For tonight."

"Forever."

She shook her head, sending autumn curls swishing across shoulders lightly dusted with freckles. "What if I don't believe in 'forever'?"

"Ah, but you are a dreamer. And dreamers always believe in forever."

"And fairy tales?"

"Those, too."

She opened her mouth, prepared to deny. He placed a finger there, swept past any and all of her objections, played on the power between them that seemed unbreakable.

"You feel so good in my arms. Do you know how beautiful you are?"

"No."

"You're stunning." He almost smiled at the way her breath hitched, at the way her head ducked. She was a goddess and the best part about it was that she didn't even realize it. "I may be the luckiest man in Monte Carlo."

"You may be the smoothest talker in Monte Carlo."

"You doubt me?" He took the rose from her fingers, brushed it across her cheek, marveled at the way her lips parted as if she could taste its fragrance, as if the smallest thing could delight her.

"Maybe a little."

He brought his lips a mere breath away from hers. "I know this sounds crazy, but I think I should warn you, I intend to marry you."

He felt her jolt, felt the rapid rise and fall of her chest against his shirtfront.

Her voice was a bare whisper. "I feel it, too, Joseph. Whatever this is that's between us. Magic—"

"Destiny."

Her gaze locked onto his. "But I don't need promises."

"I'm willing to give them."

"I'm not in a position to accept. Just give me now. Tonight."

"Ah, *querida*, yes. As a beginning."

His lips closed over hers and Briana ceased to think. It was too much, and not nearly enough. With his lips and tongue and fingertips, he seduced her. Worshiped her. He made her feel cherished and alive, both subdued and wild.

Unaccountably, tears backed up in her throat. The sensations he created with just a simple, featherlight touch were exquisite, unbearably so.

She felt the cushions of the sofa behind her knees without realizing they'd moved. He drew back, framed her face with his palms, celebrated her womanhood with the mere power of his dark gaze.

Weak, Briana sank onto the sofa, her heart beating like a runaway train. He bent down and removed her strappy gold sandals. Briana felt a moment of unease. Her feet were her least attractive feature. Yet he massaged them through the silk of her stockings, ran his palms up her calves, made her feel petite and fragile, like a world-class beauty.

Need built like steam in a pressure cooker, hot and explosive. She felt her back ease into the cushions, felt her eyes drift closed, marveled at the sensations created by his single-minded touch.

The material of his tuxedo pants brushed against her legs as he rose. Anticipation took flight like the delicate wings of a hummingbird.

*Oh, yes, now,* she thought, then frowned when he stepped behind her. Didn't he realize she'd already said yes? Accepted the journey?

He stood behind the plush sofa, gently tilted her head back to rest against the pillowed fabric.

"Relax. Let me pamper you. Ease your worries."

Briana groaned, unable to relax, wondering what good deed she'd done to deserve such exquisite treatment.

The fingertips of his left hand skimmed the curve of her neck, so lightly, in a butterfly touch, then rested beneath her upturned chin. His right hand combed through her hair, sending a burst of chills up her spine. Softly, reverently, he leaned over her and brushed his lips to her forehead.

The tenderness, the utterly focused attention on her pleasure was the most devastating gift he could have given her. Especially now, when her life felt so out of control, so chaotic.

There was no hesitation in his touch, no testing to see what she liked. He simply knew.

"You're trembling," he murmured against her brow. "Too fast for you?"

"Way too fast."

He paused.

"Don't stop," she whispered, her neck arching in surrender.

Without breaking the contact of his sure touch, he

came around the sofa, lifted her into his arms. Her breath snagged. She hadn't been carried in a man's arms since she was a child.

"There's no need—"

"Shh." His steps never faltered as he moved through the suite toward the bedroom, nor did his breath indicate that carrying her was a laborious act.

He paused just inside the doorway of the bedroom. "I'd like to tell you I'd be happy to talk the night away, but at this point I think it would be untrue. Tell me now if this is not what you want."

"You can't imagine how much I *do* want it...even though I shouldn't." The bold words heated her skin. She started to duck her head against his neck.

"Shh." He brought his mouth to hers, sending her into a wash of desire, pleasure swimming giddily in her head.

Cool sheets touched the backs of her thighs. He laid her on the satin quilt and followed. Now there were breathless murmurs, and sighs, the thud of racing hearts as they touched and pressed and learned. She caressed his chest through the silk of his tuxedo shirt, felt the wild beat that matched her own, experienced a moment of power that she could affect him so.

With exquisite care he undressed her. She wanted to return the favor but didn't trust her shaking fingers to accomplish the task. In silence she watched him, only looking away when the sight of his well-formed, bronze body threatened her sanity.

One entire wall of the room was of glass. A skylight let in the light of the moon, creating an ambience of romance. For tonight she was glad he hadn't turned on the lamps. The play of shadows created from the heavens was enough. She was afraid if she saw too much, she would never again have any peace.

Because this was only one night out of her life. The only such night that she could allow.

He seemed to sense her thoughts. Fresh nerves crowded in her throat as he eased down beside her, studying her with an intensity that sent her blood speeding through her veins. The heat of his skin against hers was like fire, the cool satin beneath her a sharp contrast.

"What troubles you, *querida?*" he asked softly.

She shook her head, hooked her hand behind his neck and drew his lips to hers. "It doesn't matter," she whispered against his mouth.

Joseph watched her eyes close, knew somehow that it *did* matter. Something was threatening this beautiful woman, twisting her insides into turmoil. He wanted to know what those secrets were, promised himself he would find out, find a way to repair whatever it was that caused her green eyes to grow distant and wary.

For now, though, he could only feel. And he was determined that she, too, would feel. Everything he had to give, and more if it was possible. She tasted like heaven, Joseph thought. He wanted to go slowly, discover her inch by fascinating inch, to savor each flavor and texture and contrast. He wasn't absolutely certain he could wait.

He fought to keep his hands from taking too greedily, fought to keep his pace and his emotions easy, fought to steady fingers that suddenly wanted to tremble.

He'd never been so in tune to a woman—so turned on, so intensely nervous. So determined that his lady share the fierceness, the fire.

"We will not hurry," he vowed in a voice that rasped like sandpaper, praying he didn't say the words in vain. His hands skimmed over her delicate skin, teased the outsides of her breasts, rested over her slightly rounded stomach. She wasn't a small woman and he found that incredibly erotic. She was soft in all the right places, firm where it counted.

"I've had all night to wonder." He spoke the words against her cheek, taking a moment to appreciate the delicate shell of her ear, to test the pearl of her earring with his tongue. "All night to imagine what your skin would feel like."

He felt her muscles quiver beneath his touch, heard her soft moan. Need, outrageous and keen, slammed through him. He buried his face in her fragrant hair, kept a firm grip on his control, gentled her when her restless limbs shifted against satin, brushed against him.

Her hips arched, helpless and seeking. Joseph took a deep breath, watched desire transform her, marveled at the contrast of his olive skin as his hand pressed against the creamy white of her stomach.

"Please," she whispered, shattering something inside him.

Good intentions evaporated. His hands roamed over her, and when simple touch wasn't enough, he used his mouth—tasting, caressing, worshiping.

Briana reached for him, unable to grasp a single sensation for longer than an instant. His lips and hands swept a path of fire unlike any she could have imagined. She felt weightless, almost like floating. The very air surrounding them shimmered with sensation, adding an ethereal dimension to the euphoria. Then that air took on an edge, like a razor-sharp knife heated beneath the rays of a scorching desert sun. She returned his touch, his kisses, hoarding the sensations, the impressions, the memories.

Lips clung as their bodies pressed. Faint tremors whispered along sensitized skin like taut live wires, the hum of desire buzzing in her head. Dark, desperate needs coiled in her belly, making her dizzy. She wanted to beg, yet didn't know what to beg for.

Each new sensation rolled over her, snatching her breath. Her skin was slick with perspiration, as was his. She felt the slide of his chest against the fullness of her breasts, breasts so sensitized they almost hurt.

"No more, Joseph!"

He understood that she wasn't asking him to stop.

"Look, *querida*. Watch me."

Tears backed up in her throat as she held his intense gaze. She saw her own desperate need reflected in his deep brown eyes. Slowly, exquisitely, he entered her, still holding her with his eyes.

She moaned, might even have whimpered. She wasn't sure. He filled her, rocked her, sent her spiraling into a stunning climax before she could even draw a breath.

She closed her eyes, images of love painted behind her lids. For endless moments she felt as if they'd actually touched the edge of heaven. She felt his breath quicken, felt a burst of blinding light behind her closed eyes as sensation welled again, flooding her, frightening her, thrilling her. She cried out, dimly aware of the husky words of Spanish he uttered, dimly aware of his own shouted release.

Acutely aware that this small slice of paradise was all that she could allow.

She'd taken something for herself tonight and hoped to God the sweetness of these few precious hours would not haunt her for the rest of her life.

Because the bizarre reality of what she could not explain was still with her. She would not, could not drag this wonderful, tender man into her private hell.

## Chapter Three

When Joseph woke up alone, his heart twisted in panic.

He'd kissed destiny last night. He knew that as surely as he knew the sun rose in the east.

Secrets, he thought, remembering the distance he'd seen in her eyes.

*I'm not in a position to accept promises.*

But he'd seen another emotion, too. And that emotion propelled him out of bed, drove him to reach desperately for the phone book on the nightstand.

"Duvaulle," he said aloud, searching the listings. He plowed his fingers through his hair in frustration. There was no listing for that name in Monte Carlo or in any of the surrounding cities that the book covered.

He reached for the phone. His first thought was to call Max. As well as a bodyguard, Max was a hell of a bloodhound. If someone needed finding, Max could find them.

But Joseph was reluctant to involve his own people. He'd found the perfect woman last night. He wanted more time to savor the feelings without questions and reminders of duty.

She was his destiny. His future. The woman he'd been searching for all his life.

Yet she'd vanished like smoke, making him wonder if he'd dreamed her.

His tuxedo pants lay crumpled on the floor where he'd stepped out of them, reminding him that it wasn't a dream, after all. He picked them up and took out his wallet.

Lifting the telephone receiver, he dialed the number on the embossed business card. The second most likely person to locate Crystal Duvaulle would be Jean-Claude, the host of last night's heart-fund charity.

UGLY MODERN APARTMENTS crowded the outskirts of Antibes while stately, seventeenth-century homes climbed the terraced hillsides as if competing with one another for a view of the sea.

Joseph wound the rented Mercedes convertible along the narrow streets of the quaint little village just opposite Nice, checking address numbers.

The villa surprised him. Its unique architecture of stucco and tile and stone pavers had set somebody back a few francs. He hadn't thought Crystal could afford something like this. Yet what did he really know of her, other than that she dreamed of travel, smelled like fresh-picked raspberries, and tasted like every one of his dreams?

He pulled into the driveway and shut off the engine, noticing that the pavers continued on to what looked like guest quarters at the back of the house. Vines of bougainvillea and white jasmine hung from trellises along the courtyard. The stone pathway leading to the front door was bordered by dense foliage and fragrant blossoms, with pineapples sprouting at will between the bases of the shrubs.

It had taken him nearly a week to track down Crystal Duvaulle's whereabouts because Jean-Claude had been out of town. Now his impatience to see her—his need to know why she'd run—was almost overwhelming.

He pressed the bell, inciting a riot of yapping from a dog.

"Peppe, hush," a woman said an instant before the door opened. She wore tailored slacks and a shimmering top that exposed a good portion of her middle. Her hair was a tumble of wheat blonde around a heart-shaped face.

She smiled and scooped up the teacup poodle who yapped incessantly. "*Bonjour.* Can I help you?"

Joseph grinned at the sight of the little dog perched in the woman's palm, a red bow in its hair, the miniature body trembling like a flimsy leaf in a windstorm. He didn't think he'd ever seen an animal that small.

"I hope so," he said, turning his attention to the woman. "I'm looking for Crystal Duvaulle. I was told she lived here."

"*Oui.* I do."

"Of course. But I am looking for Crystal."

"And you have found her."

"Where?"

Amused exasperation tilted her lips. "Right here. *I'm* Crystal Duvaulle."

"No."

She laughed, reminding him of another. "*Oui.*

Shall I produce my picture identification for the proof?''

He shook his head. ''That is not what I meant. I met a woman last week—Crystal, she said—yet you are clearly not her.''

The woman with the tousled hair and impish smile studied him for several long seconds. ''Tell me, what did this woman who shares my name look like?''

The image was as clear as if she'd been standing before him. ''About five-eight, autumn hair—more red than brown, shoulder length with soft curls. Green eyes that speak of eloquence, a laugh that begs one to participate, freckles sprinkled on her shoulders...'' His inward gaze snapped back to reality. *Dios,* he sounded like a sap.

He shoved his hands into the pockets of his slacks. ''I am sorry to have bothered you. Obviously my informant was incorrect.'' He turned to go, feeling an emptiness reminiscent of a week ago.

''Wait, *monsieur.*''

He paused, looked back. The little dog still shook like a nervous fur ball.

''Perhaps there are two of us with this same name and you have just...happened upon the wrong one. The consulate would have a complete listing. I can provide you with their number if you would like.''

''Yes. That would be appreciated.'' Joseph felt hope inch up a notch. Why hadn't he thought of that sooner? Probably because he wasn't used to doing his own detective work.

The woman disappeared, then came back, holding a slip of paper. ''Why don't you just place the call from here? If you want to, of course. I find that I am intensely curious to know if I have a namesake along the Côte d'Azur.''

"Thank you. That is very gracious of you." He followed her through the villa, noticing the elegantly tasteful furniture, the drafting table placed to catch the light from the windows, architectural designs unrolled along its surface.

The teacup poodle, set on the floor by its mistress, charged forward at full speed and ran smack into Joseph's heel, nearly sending him to the floor. Having done this, the little dog had the audacity to bark at him.

"Oh, Peppe," Crystal scolded. "Must you always blame others for your mistakes?"

Joseph looked from the angry little dog to its mistress. "He is blaming me for the mishap? Is it possible he is hurt?" The ferocious beast wasn't much bigger than a rodent. Joseph knelt and scooped the tiny fluff ball into his palm.

"No, he is not hurt," she said. "He will pout, though. You see, Peppe is without eyesight. He knows the house like braille, and we must be careful not to move the furniture around or create obstacles he is not prepared for."

"The obstacle being me?" Joseph didn't think anybody had ever accused him of being an obstacle. This incognito stuff was starting to get interesting.

"Sorry, but yes."

Her grin reminded him of *his* Crystal. And it reminded him of his desperation to find her. He set Peppe on the floor, picked up the telephone receiver and dialed, and had a ridiculous urge to cross his fingers—

"Consulate, how may I help?"

"I'm in love," he blurted, then rolled his eyes at the unconscious impulsiveness of saying what was on his brain. *Dios,* he was a grown man of thirty, not some callow youth.

The woman on the other end of the line appeared to share his sentiments. Her breath hissed out. "Oh, criminy. Has the whole Continent gone mad? What is this? An epidemic?"

Joseph wasn't sure if his heart continued to beat. For an instant it seemed to still, then it started up again at a gallop.

That voice.

A voice he would know anywhere. "Crystal?"

Dead silence greeted his query. Then abruptly, "Wrong number." A dial tone buzzed in his ear.

Very carefully he replaced the receiver. "I don't think so," he muttered softly and turned to the blond Crystal Duvaulle who was watching him with avid expectation.

Too avid, he decided.

"Well?" she asked. "What did she say?"

"She said I had the wrong number. I am curious, though. What would make you assume that the employee I was speaking with was female?"

A guilty flush stained her cheeks. Even the damned dog trembled at his tone, a tone that had commanded the attention of arrogant heads of states on more than one occasion.

"I thought so," he said and sat down on an antique velvet settee, crossed an ankle over his knee. "I would like answers, *s'il vous plaît.*"

BRIANA HEADED STRAIGHT for the guest quarters when she got home from work. Her nerves were frayed and she wasn't up to conversation right now. She'd just been laid off from her job at the consulate due to political downsizing. Great. Especially now, when money could very well become an issue.

On top of that, one of her last calls of the day had been from Joseph.

How had he found her? Oh, how she'd wanted to admit who she was, had almost done so in a burst of impulsiveness, but she'd hung up on him instead, her emotions taking her on a roller-coaster ride of giddy hope and black despair. What a mess.

Peppe darted out the doggy door, did his business where he always did, then darted back in, never even realizing she was three feet away.

She almost made it to the door of her apartment. She should have known Murphy's Law was alive and well as far as her life was concerned.

"Do not think you can sneak past me, cousin."

Briana sighed, noticing Crystal standing in the back doorway. "I'm not sneaking. I've had a tough day."

"And I have had a visitor."

Her heart lurched. So that was how he'd found her. She played dumb. "Oh? Who?"

"Perhaps you would like to tell me? He is—how was it that client from the States put it? Ah, yes. One tall drink of water. Joseph, I think his name was."

Briana knew her cousin wasn't about to let her off the hook. She pushed her hair behind her ears, hoisted the strap of her purse over her shoulder and went to join Crystal in the kitchen. "Thanks a lot for spilling your guts to a total stranger. You might have asked my permission first.''

Crystal ignored the reproach. ''You did not tell me you had met someone.''

''I haven't seen you.''

''You have been avoiding me this past week. Would that, perhaps, have something to do with the fact that you did not arrive home until dawn after the benefit I made you attend?''

''What is this? Were you spying?''

Crystal laughed. ''With Franco away on business, I must live vicariously through you, cousin. Besides, I am still pouting that I missed the benefit. Being a lowly architect, it is not often that such an invitation passes into my hands.''

''You're a brilliant architect, and you know it,'' Briana defended. ''And I'm beginning to wish you *had* gone instead of me.''

''Somehow, I do not believe you. Now, tell me all of the details. And do not leave out a single morsel of the spice.''

Briana rested her forehead in her palm. ''Oh, Crystal, you won't believe what I did. *I* can't believe what I did. It's just that—'' She jumped up, filled a glass with tap water, and stared at the murky liquid. ''Do you believe in love at first sight?''

Crystal shrugged. ''I suppose it is not impossible.''

''Oh, but it is.'' She dumped the water down the sink.

''I am lost. Why is it impossible when you ask me if it is so?''

''It's impossible for me.'' Briana placed a palm on her stomach, noticed Crystal's slight wince. It should have been Crystal celebrating the joy of pregnancy. Crystal, who feared she could not conceive, and would not accept her beau's proposal of marriage until she could be certain.

"I'm sorry, Crystal. I know this is hard on you. Believe me, if I could transfer this baby to your womb, I'd do it."

"I know, Bri. Do not fret over me."

Briana shoved her hair out of her face. "I swear I feel like I'm going mad."

"No memories have come back to you?"

"No." Because of Crystal's desperation to have a baby, Briana had allowed her cousin to drag her to that absurd fertility rock, agreed to accompany her cousin to the hot springs where people prayed for bundles of joy. She'd thought the outing was ridiculous, but had gone for Crystal's sake.

The problem was, Briana had taken an antihistamine that morning. Obviously whatever was in the exotic drink they'd served by the springs—a potion, she suspected, containing a shot of pure, lethal alcohol—had not interacted well with the medication.

Briana's only memory was of arriving at the springs. From there, the rest of the day was a total blank—until the next morning, when she woke up in her own bed, the sheets looking like a wrestling match had taken place in them, the front door standing wide open.

What the hell had she done? And *whom* had she done it with?

At the time, she hadn't worried too much about the memory lapse—until her annual physical examination. Briana had thought her frequent trips to the bathroom were caused by a common infection, perhaps even picked up at the hot springs.

She hadn't been prepared for the results of the urinalysis that had arrived in the mail not three days later.

The notice was still sitting on her dresser, a slip of paper she'd avoided as though it were a rattler coiled to strike—a notice urging her to make an appointment to begin prenatal care.

Dear God. How could her life have gotten into such a mess? It was too bizarre to even consider. Yet consider, she must.

Because whatever she'd done that day—with heaven knows whom—had altered her whole life.

It was the sole reason she couldn't act on the incredible feelings she had for Joseph Castillo.

How could she tell him she'd made love with him and yet hadn't bothered to tell him she was pregnant with another man's baby?

Briana sighed and sat down at the table.

"You have not yet told me of your night in Monte Carlo," Crystal reminded.

Joseph's image swam in her mind, his incredibly tender touch, his smooth voice and sexy accent.

"It was the wildest thing, Crystal." She traced the pattern of bright blue tulips on the Italian tiles inlaid in the oak tabletop. "I dropped the invitation and he saw it. He thought I was you—of course, he didn't really *know* you—and I let him think it. I was tired of being me that night, and wanted, *needed* the distraction."

"And your Joseph. He was the distraction?"

"He's not *my* anything."

Crystal chastized with an arched eyebrow.

"Oh, all right. He was mine...for one night. Is that so bad? He's perfect, Crystal. A fantasy. But that's all. Just a fantasy."

"Why can he not be more?"

"You know why."

"The baby?"

Briana nodded.

"Perhaps he will understand."

"How could he? *I* don't even understand."

"You are ashamed."

"No," she said immediately, then breathed out a sigh. "Maybe. I feel like a rat admitting that to you. Especially to you."

"You do not want the baby?"

Briana placed a palm over her stomach. The thought of a child made something inside her soften. But it changed everything.

She'd promised her father she would see the world for him. Her father, who was confined to a wheelchair after a fall from a ladder—a ladder he'd climbed in search of a travel book to show Briana. She'd blamed herself for that fall. Yet Thomas Duvaulle had not. He'd continued teaching, continued his duties as father to her and the three kids still at home.

Now it looked as though Briana would let him down. With a baby on the way, how would she accomplish her dream? She still had the money he'd given her—"investment in dreams," he'd said. She'd made enough through various jobs so she hadn't had to dip into the funds.

She'd been saving it, waiting for the right opportunity to come along, the right opportunity to put the money to its best use.

She'd waited too long for opportunity to knock. Now, life would take her in a different direction.

"Bri?"

"I'm still adjusting to the idea of a baby, trying to make some sense out of the circumstances. It's like— I don't know how to explain it. The void in my memory is so scary. The shame is from not knowing what I did— Well, at least, how I acted when I did it."

Crystal laughed, effectively lightening the atmosphere. It was one of the things Briana loved most about her cousin. Her innate enjoyment of life, her ability to laugh with and at and around any situation. A trait that Briana shared—most of the time.

"I have had a strange thought, and you will think that I, too, am mad," Crystal said, her giggle inviting and contagious.

"Well, don't keep it to yourself. Misery loves company, and like Noah's ark, I'm happiest when I do things in twos—including going insane."

"Oh, it is odd that you have mentioned the great ark." Crystal laughed again and crossed herself in the traditional Catholic gesture. "The Virgin Mary is perhaps frowning at the moment, but have you made the connection with your quirky baby conception and your Joseph?"

Briana opened her mouth, snapped it shut, then burst out laughing. "Don't *even* finish that thought. We'll both be struck by lightning! I'm no Virgin Mary and Joseph is... Well, he's almost too good to be true, but he's definitely not... " She searched for the right word, couldn't come up with it and went off into another peal of laughter.

"Criminy, Crystal. Immaculate conception? No way. I've got way too many sins on my head. You're as crazy as I am!"

Crystal shrugged. "You ask for explanations to the unexplainable."

"Well, not that one."

"I like it," Crystal continued like a dog with a bone. "Would that not be a grand story?"

"For the tabloids," Briana grumbled. They'd done a lot of this as kids—taken a silly notion and batted it back and forth, spinning it into a fairy-tale story. The details had never been this personal, though, or this nerve-racking.

"And your Joseph is very likely Catholic," Crystal added without pause. "That is the predominant faith of Spain, I think."

"He's not my Joseph. And how do you know he's from Spain?"

"He told me, of course. Actually, he said it was off the coast of Spain. A place called Valldoria. You do not think I would give away your whereabouts to a stranger without getting a little information on him, do you?"

"Yes. Being in love with Franco has made you soft in the head."

"Then we are in the same boat, after all."

Briana started to deny, but wasn't sure what she was actually protesting—that they were both insane or both in love.

She didn't *even* want to entertain that last thought,

and was saved from further speculation when the doorbell rang.

"I'll catch that," Briana said. "Then I'm going back to my apartment and soak in a hot tub." She nearly tripped over Peppe as he raced her for the door. "Peppe, stop that barking. You can't see a blessed thing, so why do you insist on going to the door?"

She scooped up the dog and pulled open the door.

And nearly dropped the teacup poodle.

"*Bonjour, mademoiselle.* I am Joseph Castillo. And you are...?"

Her breath stilled in her throat. She felt like a ninny, but for the life of her, she couldn't find her voice.

He reached for her hand, drew her knuckles to his lips. "It appears we are destined to celebrate intimacies before introductions."

Briana stared at him, her heart in her mouth and blurted, "Please tell me you're not Catholic."

# Chapter Four

"Pardon?" Joseph's brows snapped together. "What do my religious preferences have to do with proper—or improper—introductions?"

"Forget it. You don't want to know."

She waved her free hand in a dismissive gesture, her gaze skittering away as though it was too painful for her to keep looking at him.

"I get the feeling that I do," he said softly. "But we will leave that for another time. Why did you run from me, *querida*?"

"I'm not your darling."

"Ah, but I suspect you are my beloved. Will you tell me your true name now?" He saw the hesitation, the surrender.

Her breath hissed out on a sigh. "Briana."

"And Duvaulle?"

She gave a small shrug. "That's mine."

"Briana." He tested the name, found that he liked it. Very much. "It suits you."

"How do you know? You don't even know me."

The look he gave her caused her breath to hitch.

Good. He definitely felt off-balance here and didn't want to be the only one in such a state.

"Perhaps not your true given name until this moment, but I definitely know you. If you recall, I expressed intentions of marriage."

She shook her head. "Men often say that when they want to get a woman in bed."

"Shame on you, *querida*." His fingers itching with the need to touch her, he reached out and softly brushed her cheek. "And if memory serves me, that was not an issue at the time."

"Meaning I'd already proved how easy I was?"

"No. Never easy. Right. Perfect. But never easy."

"Thank you—I think."

"Why did you find it necessary to deceive me with your name?"

She shrugged. "You're the one who made assumptions."

"Assumptions you neglected to correct. Is there somewhere we can go to speak? In private." He looked past her to where Crystal was shamelessly eavesdropping.

"*Bonjour, Mademoiselle Duvaulle.*"

"*¡Hola! Señor Castillo.*"

He grinned. "I see language fluency runs in the family."

"As well as insanity," Briana muttered and thrust Peppe at Crystal. "Let's get out of here before you catch it, too."

She brushed by him, went through the courtyard and disappeared around the corner, obviously assuming he would just follow. Joseph got a firm hold on his astonishment. He kept forgetting she didn't know of his title, that he was used to people bowing in his presence, that he was used to being the first to dismiss or leave a room.

He followed her, noticing that she did at least wait by the doorway of the guest apartment. He noticed, too, that her hand trembled on the doorknob.

He preceded her through the doorway, and took a moment to look at the surroundings. Pots of flowers and greenery rested on every available surface, reminding him of a greenhouse decorated with furniture—the furniture complementing the flora instead of the other way around.

Vivid splashes of color drew his eye at every turn, from the art on the walls to the wild throw pillows on the overstuffed sofa.

Homey. Quaint. Happy, just like Briana's laughter. Nothing somber or austere or palatial in sight.

"Who did your decorating?"

"The apartment belongs to Franco—Crystal's fiancé—as does the house we were just in. This place came mostly furnished. I added the plants and fussy stuff."

He grinned. "I like the fussy stuff. Have you lived here long?"

"About six months."

"So, Crystal is the cousin who invited you to stay when the Paris modeling caused you to starve." He stroked the spidery leaf of a fern.

She rolled her eyes. "Nobody looking at me could accuse me of starving."

His gaze locked onto hers, deceptively lazy, profoundly sensual. Riveting. "I'm looking at you. What I see is a goddess."

She reached for the back of the couch to steady herself. "I have a weakness for flattery. I wish you wouldn't hand it out so easily."

"You inspire it. It is the truth."

"Whatever. It makes my job of brushing you off harder."

His hand stilled against the plant leaf, his voice taking on an edge that made his accent more pronounced. "You intend to brush me off?"

"Yes. No." Briana wiped her damp palms on her hips. She didn't mean to hurt him, was a little surprised that she could. She drew in a breath, and looked toward the tiny kitchen. "Do you want some tea? Coffee?" *Me?* she nearly said.

"Coffee, if it is not too much trouble."

"No trouble." She escaped to the kitchen, feeling alternately thrilled that he was here after all, and terrified at the same time. How did a woman go about carrying on a conversation with a man she'd been intimate with on such a short acquaintance?

A man she was in love with. A love that had no hope. That could never go anywhere.

Lordy, she'd thought her life was in a mess before. Now it was painfully chaotic.

"You are nervous. Why is that?"

Briana barely suppressed a scream when he spoke from right at her elbow. She caught the lid of the tea canister before it hit the tile countertop. "Please, don't sneak up on me like that!"

"I did not sneak. You were aware that I was in the house."

"In the front room. Not the kitchen."

"I am finding it is not wise to allow you too far

out of my sight. For all I know, you will disappear out the back door.''

"And if I did?"

"I would follow."

Just that simply. "Joseph..."

"Do not look at me like that. You would want me to follow."

Yes, she would. But she *shouldn't* want it. She poured coffee into a mug decorated with spring flowers, handed it to him, then dropped a tea bag in her own cup of hot water and added a dash of honey. Someone had told her caffeine wasn't good for expectant women. It would be a tough vice to give up.

She moved to the kitchen table. "Do you want to sit?"

He hooked an ankle around the leg of a chair and sat, his penetrating dark gaze so focused on her it made her squirm.

"I wish you wouldn't do that," she muttered.

"Do what?"

"Look at me like that."

"Like the sun rises and sets just for your benefit?"

Oh, dear heaven. How could she harden her heart against such poetry. "Do you have a whole list?"

"Of what?"

"Pretty lines.

"No lines, Briana. I've told you, I intend to—"

"Marry me, yes." She waved her hand in dismissal and tried to suppress the jolt of longing his mere presence inspired. She'd made love with this man, and the image of that incredible night held center court in her mind, making it difficult to meet his gentle gaze.

"That makes you uncomfortable."

"It helps if two people are of the same mind on the subject."

"No matter. I am confident of my powers of persuasion. The pursuit is half the fun."

Her hands went still against the china cup. "This is a game to you?"

"No. I've never been more serious about anything in my life."

She groaned, partly because she could tell he spoke the truth, and partly because she could not accept that truth. "Please. I'm not what you think—"

"Then tell me what you are. Who you are."

"I can't."

He watched her, reached out and brushed the back of his knuckles against her cheek. "Nothing is that bad, *querida*."

"How would you know? You're a man."

"And glad of it."

His suggestive tone and heated look nearly took her breath away. Memories of passion and whisper-soft touches swam in her mind. "That was a mistake."

"Making love?"

"Yes."

He appeared to mull over something, then came to a decision. "You may be right."

Her heart sank. Saying it and having it confirmed were two different things. "Good. I'm glad we got that straight. So now—"

"You are a woman who deserves to be wooed."

Her throat snapped closed. She'd thought they were going to agree to part. "Wooed?" she parroted. Perversely, happiness surged through her.

"Yes. At any cost."

Sidetracked now, she repeated, "Any cost?"

"Any."

"Can you afford me?" Oh, that sounded terrible.

He didn't appear to take offense. He grinned. "I can give it my best shot. Are you expensive?"

She shook her head, and sighed. "This conversation is ridiculous. Even if you were as rich as the Rockefellers, I can't be bought." Money would not get her out of the predicament she was in, would not change an event that had already been set in motion.

"And if I am richer?"

She laughed, glanced at his charcoal slacks and black polo shirt. "I'd say you're as big a dreamer as I am."

"So, I cannot impress you with LearJets and cruise-ship-size yachts?"

"Well, yes, you could impress me with those things—even if they do belong to the company you work for."

His brows rose. "Did I say that?"

"In so many words. But it's not *things* that make a person. It's what's inside. In here." She placed her hand over her heart.

"You were not impressed when I told you of my heart," he reminded.

Marriage, she thought. Which was out of the question. "On the contrary. I was impressed. Am impressed. But you'll have to forgive me for not trusting."

"I understand. It is too soon."

"Or too late."

"Why would you say that?" He reached for her hands, took them in his. "What is hurting you?"

"Nothing."

"That, I cannot accept."

"You'll have to."

"Would it be so difficult to give me the opportunity to change your mind?"

"Even if I wanted to let you change my mind, I *can't.*" She jumped up from the table, took a deep breath when emotions threatened to get the better of her.

Her gaze out the kitchen window slammed into the face of her neighbor. Her heart lurched in panic as he grinned and gave her a jaunty wave. The carpenter had been doing a lot of that lately—lurking around, leering at her as if he were the cat who'd swiped the canary.

He had a bushy goatee that hung from his face like a squirrel's tail and a belly that would give Santa Claus a run for his money. It all but hid the tool belt that threatened to drag his pants down his hips. The man gave her the creeps.

Surely she hadn't—not with *him!*

"Oh, Lord," she groaned and whirled around.

"What is it?"

"Nothing." Nerves and sick dread swamped her. Why the hell couldn't she remember what she'd done? Whom she'd done it with? The idea that it was the carpenter didn't bear thinking about.

Joseph rose and looked past her out the window. "Do you know the workman who is next door?"

"No." At least, she hoped not.

"But his presence somehow bothers you."

She shook her head. "I'm just being silly. Everything's in a mess right now. I lost my job today. I've got to make some plans. Everything is overwhelming me.''

"You lost your job? Did my calling you there create trouble?"

"It's nothing to do with you. Or me. The department's downsizing. I got caught in the cross fire."

"If this job is important to you, I have a certain amount of pull and can get you restored."

His utter assurance made her smile. She remembered his description of himself when she'd asked him what kind of work he did. "The ambassador of goodwill at work?"

"Something like that." He sipped coffee, glanced around the room. "Shall I use my diplomacy and smooth the way?"

"No. I'm used to doing my own smoothing. Besides, the position wasn't a career—just a temporary job I took, figuring it might turn into something that would involve travel. No big deal."

"So, what will you do?"

She shrugged. "Find something else." And quickly, she hoped.

"You could model."

She laughed. "Are you kidding? I'd have to drop fifteen pounds." An impossibility when she would soon be putting on *more* weight. Just the thought made her heart pound in anxiety. "I don't have that kind of time or dedication any more. I need a job now. Not six months from now." *When she could be a maternity model!*

"Do not sell yourself short, Briana."

"I'm not. I'm being realistic. But you're sweet to

encourage. Don't worry, something will come along.''

"Let me take you away."

"I can't go away. Damn it, Joseph—"

"Not away in that manner. Just for the night. To take your mind off your troubles."

"I did that last week. With you. Look how that turned out."

"Very well, in my opinion."

"We can't repeat that night, Joseph."

"Because of your employment position?"

"No. Because... Just because."

"Fine. No intimacies, I promise. But let me ease your worries tonight. Let's have an evening where no everyday troubles intrude."

Oh, that sounded like heaven. But would she just be getting herself in deeper? Allowing herself to fall harder for this man? She glanced out the window. The carpenter was still grinning and waving like a fool.

"Where did you have in mind?"

"Dinner. Aboard my boat."

"You mean your cruise ship?"

"We can cruise if you like."

She shook her head. "I don't think that's such a good idea."

"You are worried about being alone with me? We will be well chaperoned. There is a full staff aboard the boat."

"How many is a full staff?"

"It is a big yacht."

It was too tempting by far to taste the edge of heaven Joseph offered. Still, a night out might be nice. At least until that goofy carpenter went home for the day.

"I have a better idea," she said. "There's a place up in the hills. It'll be fun."

SHE'D CHANGED INTO A georgette skirt in a reptile print and paired it with a bulky Shaker-stitch tunic sweater in gray. The outfit spelled *femininity* in capital letters and Joseph could barely take his eyes off her.

The night had turned chilly, but Briana had urged him to keep the top down on the Mercedes. He loved the way she shook her head in the wind, never complaining about it mussing her hair. She laughed and reached her hands toward the sky.

"There must be a million stars out tonight. Riding like this, I feel as if I can touch them all."

Joseph smiled and negotiated a switchback turn on the Grande Corniche road. "What would you do with one if you could reach it?"

"Put it in my pocket and save it for a rainy day."

He frowned and she laughed at him. People rarely laughed at him.

"The song, Joseph. Don't you remember it? 'Catch a falling star and put it in your pocket'?"

"I must have missed that one."

"What, have you been locked away on a desert island?"

Close, he thought. A place where expectations were high and privacy was impossible. Where loneliness had nearly smothered him. He didn't tell her any of this, though, and she didn't seem to expect an answer, anyway. Besides, there would be time to tell her all about his country. For tonight, and for the next three weeks, he intended to concentrate on Briana. On wooing her. Getting her to fall in love with him.

She was perfect for him. He'd never felt so strongly about anything or anyone in his life.

He would have to break through a few of her barriers, but he felt he was up to the task. Especially because it was so important to him. His future, every day for the rest of his life, depended upon his success.

It took more than an hour to reach the restaurant in the hills. Nestled in a ravine and surrounded by lush vegetation, he would have missed it, had Briana not been directing the way.

He'd barely shut off the engine before Briana swung her sexy legs out of the car. He would have opened the door if she'd have given him half a chance. Scarcely allowing him time to pocket the keys, she linked their arms and tugged him inside.

The place was like nothing in his experience. Unpretentious, simple and fun. And noisy. A place where Briana fit in as if she'd been born there.

"Hi, Claudette," she greeted the hostess, her hips already picking up the rhythm of the live music vying with the sounds of reveling customers. "I've brought a novice with me tonight. Be sure and give him the special treatment."

Grinning, Claudette nodded. Joseph's brow furrowed.

"A novice, *querida?*" He spoke the words close to her ear, drew in a sharp breath when she turned and patted his cheek, laughing up at him. He wasn't sure whether to be affronted at being called a novice, or whether to simply hoist her over his shoulder and haul her out of here in search of privacy. That sunshine grin was playing havoc with his libido.

"You're in for a treat," she said, linking their fingers and sweeping him along in her effervescent wake.

He couldn't decide which to concentrate on—the rustic decor or Briana's animation.

Negotiating the dim interior of the restaurant took precedence. Wood-plank floors rang hollow beneath the heels of his loafers. Harvest tables, more like picnic benches, lined walls decorated with antique farm implements and business cards left behind by happy customers.

Briana tugged him down beside her at a table and the hostess placed two bottles of wine in front of them. A musical group playing mandolin, guitar and accordion moved about, inspiring patrons to stomp and clap and sing along. The employees appeared to be dressed in some sort of period costume, reminding him of a folk festival he'd passed through once on his way to a hospital-wing dedication.

"Friendly place," Joseph commented, wondering about the cuisine. "May we see a menu?" When the hostess merely smiled, he repeated his question in French. She made a vague gesture with her hand. He tried again in German. Same gesture, as if she were pointing out the decor and the other patrons. Both English and Italian got a similar response.

Joseph frowned and glanced at Briana, who laughed at his puzzlement.

"They don't speak," Briana informed him.

"That's absurd. Is their native language not French?"

"They're fluent in several languages...." Her voice trailed off, her face taking on a glow that made Joseph want to simply stop and stare. "Maybe I can get a job here."

"You're getting sidetracked." He noticed the hostess had walked away without providing the requested menus. "Why wouldn't that woman talk to me?"

"She was. With her hands. She was showing you what they serve by pointing out what's on the other tables. It's like pantomime, or charades. You ask a question and they act out the answer."

"I'm aware of the game."

"Good. You'll fit right in. Red or white?"

"Pardon?"

"Wine. Red or white?" Her hand hovered over the bottles.

"How do I choose when I do not know what the meal will be?"

"Oh, Joseph. You've been to too many stuffy banquets. This is a place where you let your hair down. Regardless of what we're eating, what do your taste buds ask for?"

"Raspberries. On your skin."

Her hand jerked and the bottle tipped. He caught it, never taking his eyes from hers. Their fingers brushed against the cold bottle. She snatched her hands back, tucked them in her lap.

He grinned, knew he'd gotten to her. He poured the red. It was the closest and easiest. He raised his glass to her, saw that her eyes widened as if a guilty thought had crossed her mind, saw that she barely sipped the alcohol.

"You do not like it?"

"It's fine. I'm not much of a drinker. Maybe I'll just have a soda."

He set down his glass. "It appears I'm at a loss. How do we act out 'soda'?" At any other restaurant he simply would have given a discreet nod and attentive servers would have materialized to grant his wish. But here he was unknown—and somewhat out of his depth.

She giggled. "Just ask for it. They understand you. They just won't talk back."

A waiter came to the table this time. His name tag said Nikko.

"We'd like two colas, please."

Nikko nodded his understanding and placed a wooden bowl on the table. It contained a head of lettuce, carrots with the green tops still attached, radishes straight from the plant, leaves and all, a bunch of green onions and several stalks of celery bundled with a twist tie. A lethal-looking butcher knife lay across the vegetable-garden-in-a-bowl.

"What is this?" Joseph voiced the question to no one in particular.

The waiter answered, or demonstrated, rather. The young man picked up the knife and a carrot and made chopping motions, then placed wooden salad bowls in front of them. Catching on now, Joseph frowned.

"We're supposed to *make* the salad?"

Nikko grinned and Briana clapped him on the shoulder.

"Good, Joseph."

"Thank you," he said automatically and felt a smile tug at his lips. Imagine, he thought, customers expected to do the work of servants. His father would have a fit. Joseph found he was having a ball. He thought back to the woman his family had chosen for him to marry. He tried to imagine Raquel Santiago in a place like this, but couldn't. Nor could he imagine the proper heiress tearing open a head of lettuce with such zeal as Briana did now.

Amazing how such a simple thing could entrance him so, yet everything about Briana Duvaulle delighted him.

Someone shouted Briana's name, snapping Joseph out of his trance. He looked around for the source of the interruption and caught the edge of the bench as it wobbled.

He felt as though he'd somehow missed the first act of a play. With lettuce juice dripping from her fingers, Briana hopped up and joined several of the regulars on the dance floor in a folk dance that reminded him somewhat of the bunny hop.

The salad forgotten, Joseph watched her. It took a little getting used to, this penchant she had for exiting at whim. It was a totally new experience for him, kept him on his toes and off-balance at the same time.

Something inside him swelled—both pride and excitement, and the realization that he'd finally found what he'd been searching for all his life; what he'd been missing.

*She's the one.*

People flocked to her. She had the type of personality that naturally drew others. She teased and flirted with her dance partners...and with him. She'd left him alone at the table without so much as a pardon, yet she was attentive and aware, even from a distance. Her gaze continually searched for and met his, always with a smile that made him feel warm, like he'd come home at last.

The reptile-print skirt floated around her calves as she bounced and swayed to the music, her head thrown back in laughter. The happy sound, unrestrained, could be heard above the noise of the restaurant. When she laughed, she threw herself into the experience wholeheartedly.

Joseph found himself wanting to join her. He wondered if there had ever been a time when he'd allowed his reserve to slip, to shout out in laughter with a soul-deep joy. He didn't think so, and the realization made him even more desperate to bind Briana to him, to soak up the innate goodness she radiated without even trying.

He wanted more laughter in his life.

He wanted Briana in it.

Duty and honor were important to him, but lately he'd felt smothered by tradition, felt as if a storm was raging inside him, yet he'd been helpless to calm the roiling emotions.

Falling in love with Briana Duvaulle made him feel free.

"Oh, that was so much fun," Briana said, sliding onto the bench next to him, her chest rising and falling from the exertion of the dance, drawing Joseph's interested stare. "Why didn't you join us?"

Picking up a paper napkin, he wiped cucumber juice from his hands. "There are times to participate and times when it is more fun to watch. You are a joy to watch, Briana."

Briana tucked her hair behind her ear. She'd seen Joseph watching her on the dance floor, seen the tilt of his sensual lips, the spark of amusement in his dark eyes. She'd had some reservations about bringing him here. He seemed to be fitting in just fine, though.

He still watched her, his face so close all it would take was a mere shift and their lips would touch. Oh, how she wanted to initiate that shift. Her heart pounded harder, and it wasn't from the exertion of the dance.

Nikko interrupted the moment when he set a basket of bread on the table and sliced cold cuts on their plates.

The meal was simple but tasty. The people were full of joy, bent on letting their hair down. Briana clapped and sang along, occasionally hopping up to dance. She loved engaging the waiters in their game, loved watching Joseph's reactions. He was an amazing man, proving he could wear a tux and talk politics and finance with high-powered people, yet blend in with country folk and simplicity with ease. He never commented on the scarred tables or plank floors.

When Nikko came around once more with a wooden board laden with meats, Joseph pointed to a sausage-like item that looked like brown Ping-Pong balls attached to a string.

"What are they?" he asked.

Briana bit her lip. "You don't want to know."

"Ah, now you have me curious. Besides, I quite enjoyed them. Proceed, Nikko."

Nikko went into a pantomime and Joseph fell right in with the game. "Circle," he guessed. "Sun. Round. Ball."

Nikko nodded, then became more animated.

"Oink?" Joseph asked. "Pig? Pig...ball... Pig's

balls!'' he shouted triumphantly just as Nikko brought the butcher knife down with a whack, severing the little balls.

Joseph cringed and crossed his legs.

Briana burst out laughing, the sound echoing off the walls.

Still a little horrified by what he'd been eating—and enjoying—Joseph was charmed by her gaiety. She was laughing at him and it made him feel ten feet tall. Go figure.

"I've been eating pig's balls?"

She nodded. "Still taste good?"

His eyes, smoldering with sensuality, lowered to her mouth, making her imagine things that had nothing to do with crazy pantomimes or food. Her breath suspended in her throat and for the life of her she couldn't look away.

The emotions he evoked scared the daylights out of her. He made her yearn for things she could not have. Because if he knew her secret he would surely turn away in disgust.

Or would he? she wondered. Was it just her own guilt, her own insanity that made her feel that way?

She just didn't know. What she did know was that she would rather give Joseph up before they got in any deeper, give him up before she was forced to find out his reaction.

She wanted to ask about his family; to ask about his country—what it was like, what exactly an ambassador of goodwill did. But those details would only make him more real to her.

"Why do your eyes become shadowed, *querida?*"

She shook her head. "It's been a long day. I guess I'm just tired."

"Do you want to go?"

She nodded. "Maybe it's best."

THE DRIVE HOME WAS subdued. The top was still down on the Mercedes, but Briana didn't laugh or reach for the stars. Because all the stars and wishes in the world wouldn't change her circumstances; wouldn't free her to accept what Joseph appeared to want to give.

When they pulled up in her driveway, she touched his hand before he could shut off the engine. "Don't."

He watched her in the stillness broken only by night birds calling to their mates. The smell of jasmine and cypress drifted on the gentle breeze. "I am getting a bad feeling, here. Similar to the one I experienced a week ago when I woke up alone."

"I can't do this, Joseph."

"Why? Are you promised to another?"

"It's a little late to be asking that question."

"Perhaps. I am asking now, though."

"No. I'm not involved with anyone else." *I hope.*

"Then what troubles you?"

She shook her head, wanting to unburden her soul, unable to do it. "My life is up in the air right now. It's not something I can talk about." She opened the car door before she lost her head and threw herself into his arms, where she really wanted to be. "It's better if we stop now, Joseph. It just won't work between us."

## Chapter Five

For the next week, flowers arrived daily at her doorstep. Roses of every color, rare orchids that must have cost the earth, sunny daffodils that made her smile and want to cry at the same time. This recent penchant for tears at the drop of a hat—or a delivery of daffodils—was new to her. The book she'd gotten on the stages of pregnancy said it was a natural occurrence.

The cards were pure poetry. He likened the velvet of the roses to the softness of her skin, the rarity of the orchids to her unique personality, the daffodils to her happy laughter.

Next came a carton of fresh raspberries.

The expression on the delivery boy's face matched her own curiosity. She grabbed the card, scanned it, and felt her face flame.

"Someone is courting you, no?" the young man asked, obviously hoping for a scrap of gossip to carry back to his co-workers. "Or perhaps has made a terrible faux pas and is attempting to apologize with flowers and…fruit?"

"Don't ask," she muttered, reaching for the clip-

board to sign her name. She almost felt as though she
should apologize to the kid—who had refused a tip
each of the many times he'd been to her door, stating
he'd been paid handsomely for his time. His curiosity
was mounting, though. Thank heavens, the card had
been sealed in an envelope—and had been written by
Joseph himself. She could tell because it matched the
handwriting on all the other cards.

Briana closed the door and stared down at the delicate fruit.

Never again will I smell or taste a raspberry
without thinking of the scent of your skin. You
feel it, too, do you not? I will wait for you, sweet
Briana.

Love, Joseph

Yes, she felt it. Vivid images swam in her mind;
the feel of his lips against her skin, his tongue tracing
the curve of her breasts, the sound of his soft sexy
accent as he complimented her scent, her taste.

Briana groaned and went to the kitchen to put the
berries in the refrigerator. Joseph certainly knew how
to wear a girl down. She'd never had a man be so
attentive, so persistent. The notes attached to the gifts
tapped right into her heart's desire. He knew she
wanted him, knew she was lying to herself and to
him.

He was a dream. A fantasy.

There was none of the game playing associated
with dating. None of the wondering if he would call,
or *Does he like me?* No on-your-best-behavior, put

your-best-foot-forward stuff. He'd seen her at her most vulnerable—naked, body and soul.

With Joseph Castillo, she knew where she stood. He'd told her his feelings, his intentions. He called her daily, and what he didn't say with his voice, he said with notes attached to flower deliveries and cartons of raspberries.

Briana sighed, feeling her walls of resistance crumble, unable to shore them back up. For the first time in her life, she didn't wonder if she was too tall or too plump or if her feet were too big. She didn't worry if she laughed too loud or said something dumb. Because Joseph made it clear that he *enjoyed* her, celebrated her womanhood.

Although she'd resisted, he hadn't given up. He was sure of himself, of his manhood.

In that case, could it be that he might be able to accept the fact that she carried a child? A child she could not explain?

She felt herself weakening, touched a trembling finger to the delicate bud of a peach-colored rose. She felt so uncertain, so torn.

The doorbell rang again.

"Good heavens, this has got to stop," she said aloud.

She yanked open the door and frowned. It wasn't another delivery. "Why are you ringing my doorbell, Crystal?"

"Just testing to see if the batteries need changing. The bell appears to be getting quite a bit of use lately."

"Oh, shut up and get in here."

Briana turned and went to the kitchen for yet another pitcher of water to add to the many vases decorating her tables and countertops. Keeping the blooms alive was becoming a full-time job.

Crystal trailed her, as Briana knew she would. The constant stream of delivery people was too much for Crystal's curious nature.

"It looks like a florist's shop in here."

"Yeah. I could start my own business." Actually it had given her an idea. She'd minored in horticulture in college. She could go to work in a florist's shop. It wouldn't tie in with her goal to travel, but it would pay the bills until she could find her feet, both emotionally and physically.

As she tipped the pitcher of water over a vase of orchids, Briana noticed that Crystal was craning her neck to read the cards lying on the table.

"Your Joseph is quite a poet."

"It's not nice to read other people's mail."

"Ah, but this is not mail. And it is in plain sight."

Briana set aside the water pitcher and sank onto the sofa, hugging a bright throw pillow to her stomach. "Oh, Crystal, what am I going to do?"

"I should think that is obvious. This is a man you do not want to let get away."

"What if it's not real?"

"His feelings?" Crystal's tone was clearly astonished. "Bri, the man is totally besotted with you. How can you doubt that?"

"He doesn't know me."

"Was it not you who asked about love at first sight? Must you think the situation to death?"

"Maybe I wouldn't have before."

"Before we went to the springs, you mean."

"Yes. Before I did some crazy thing with heaven-knows-who."

"Well, perhaps this is a blessing...this memory lapse. At least you don't have unpleasant visions to haunt you."

"I *want* those visions, Crystal. The not knowing is driving me insane." Not only was she steering clear of the goofy carpenter, now she was imagining the delivery boy was looking at her with familiarity. Which had a perfectly logical explanation, she told herself. The guy was at her door no less than three times a day. She definitely needed to get a grip!

"You are sounding more certain about the pregnancy than you were a month ago. Have you missed your cycle again?"

Briana nodded. When she'd had a light period last month, she'd questioned the accuracy of the test. The baby book had said that in some newly pregnant women, that would occur. A careful watch of the calendar, though, had caused her spirits to sink. This time, her period was definitely late.

"What about you?" Briana asked, aware that Franco had been in town off and on over the past month. "Any sign of the monthly curse?" A would-be blessing in Briana's case.

"No. But I cannot allow myself to hope. Besides, since I do not ovulate like normal women, I tend to forget that monthly cycles are part of life for a female."

"Are you taking the medication to bring on your period?"

Crystal shook her head. "I do not want to chance it. If by some miracle I was to become pregnant and not know it, the medication could harm a baby. Besides, I do not want to rely on pills. I want my body to work properly without the aid of drugs."

"Crystal—"

Crystal hopped up from the sofa and waved a hand in dismissal. "We must not belabor this subject. And we have gotten off track. We must decide about all these flowers."

"We?"

"Of course. Left to your own devices, you will let your Joseph slip through your fingers. I am here to urge you not to allow that to happen."

"You always were a nag."

"Yes, but I am a fun nag. Now why do you not call this man who appears to be too good to be true?"

"Because he's probably just a figment of my imagination."

"Nonsense. You are on the Riviera where love blooms like miracles. Besides, you have flowers and raspberries as proof."

Briana narrowed her eyes. "How did you know about the raspberries?"

"Peppe was out doing his business and I saw the delivery."

"You were able to see what it was from that distance?"

"Of course not, silly. I stopped the boy and looked. Now why is the man sending you fruit?"

Briana grinned. "I'm not telling."

"But of course you must," Crystal insisted.

The doorbell rang again, giving Briana an excellent excuse to keep her cousin in suspense. Besides, the significance of that particular gift was too personal to share, even with her cousin.

As Briana had suspected, the summons heralded another delivery. Except this time, by Joseph in person.

Butterflies took flight in her stomach. He wore an old Harvard sweatshirt with sleeves pushed up to the elbows, along with jeans worn white from repeated washings rather than trendy design. His rich brown hair was windswept, falling carelessly over his forehead in front and brushing the collarless shirt in back. Dirty white high-tops encased his feet. His face, characterized by the slash of his high cheekbones, was smooth-shaven and achingly handsome—and creased with such a gentle smile she could have wept.

And here she stood, having trouble drawing a decent breath, staring. She probably looked like a besotted fool.

As if in a trance, she accepted the bouquet of wildflowers he handed her.

"*Coup de foudre,*" Crystal said. Briana's head whipped around. She'd forgotten her cousin was standing behind her. "*Oui,* I believe such things are possible. *Bonjour,* Joseph. Your courtship is impressive. And I am a hard one to impress. *Au revoir,* cousin. You will remember my advice, no?" And with that, Crystal sashayed out the door, her hips swaying beneath a pair of white slacks that displayed her curves to their greatest advantage.

"What advice did she give?" Joseph asked. Most men couldn't help but stare when Crystal entered or exited a room. The sensuality was innate, not deliberate.

Joseph's gaze never left Briana.

Oh, dear. The tally of his assets didn't need boosting. Still, it went up several notches. He watched her with an indulged smile. She remembered he'd asked a question. Advice. That was it.

"Crystal gives advice on everything from mosquitoes to ball gowns." She buried her nose in the bouquet. "These are pretty. Thanks."

"You're welcome."

She parted the colorful blooms. "What, no card?"

"I prefer to deliver my words in person."

There was that tone again. The one she found so hard to resist. "Joseph…"

"I am not generally known for my patience. With you, I have exercised that trait admirably, I think. At the very least, I must deserve a medal. May I come in?"

His determination appeared to outmatch hers. She stepped back.

He moved into the room, touched the delicate throat of an orchid, stroked it as if stroking a woman. Briana swallowed hard.

"Uh, thank you for the flowers."

"You've already done that."

"For the wildflowers. Not for the rest of them." She felt a bubble of laughter and couldn't hold it back. "I doubt there's a bloom left in all of France."

His answering smile was a bit sheepish, yet oh-so-masculine. "Habit. I am used to doing things in a grand way."

"They're certainly grand…and abundant. With the plants already here, it's beginning to look like a greenhouse."

"It suits you."

"Does it?"

"Yes. I knew you were a woman who appreciated flowers when I gave you the rose that first night."

"And how did you arrive at that conclusion?" She noticed how his eyes went smoky when he mentioned that night, and wondered if her own did the same. Just in case, she ducked her head, hiding her emotions behind the fragrant blossoms clutched in her hands.

"The way you automatically bring them to your face—like now—the way you inhale their essence, the way appreciation lights your face and shines in your eyes."

"You're a smooth talker, Joseph Castillo."

"I like to think of it as determination."

She watched him walk toward her and suddenly had an irrational urge to run. Her heart drummed in her ears and her mouth went dry. Intent fairly shouted from his bronze features. This was a man who knew what he wanted and wasn't afraid to go after it. If she stood here, she wasn't sure she could be responsible for her actions. She wasn't a weak woman, Briana assured herself.

Yet, she never moved a muscle, never tried to evade when his fingertip traced the curve of her cheek. He took the flowers from her unsteady fingers and lowered his head.

"If I don't do this I will go mad." His lips covered hers with a tempered strength that spoke volumes.

He wanted her. Badly.

Just as she wanted him.

As his arms wound around her, she felt herself losing control. That was becoming a habit with this man—a habit she couldn't afford.

Unable to help herself, she leaned into him, inhaled the scent of his cologne that she smelled in her dreams; tasted the sweet, sincere promise of his lips and tongue.

He took her actions as permission and deepened the kiss, letting loose that strength of emotion she'd sensed just below his civilized surface, sweeping her away on a journey that left no room for reason or doubt.

As she had on that first night with him, she wanted. Wanted like she'd never wanted before. The ache that swelled in her chest was born of both desire and desperation.

Joseph wasn't as patient as he might have been. He wanted to experience everything at once—*needed* to with a compulsion that surprised the hell out of him. His mouth raced over her face, streaked down her throat, then returned to her lips—lips that met his with a fervor that nearly outdistanced his.

Never before had he known a woman who matched him so well. Never before had he known this gnawing desperation to brand a woman as his.

He wanted to drag her down on the overstuffed cushions of the sofa, whip that floaty feminine dress over her head until she was naked and burning beneath him.

But he also wanted her to come to him, wanted her to admit that she needed him as badly as he needed her. For a lifetime. Not just for the moment.

With a great deal of reluctance, he gentled his

hands and drew away. Her labored breathing matched his own. It took a moment for him to find his voice.

"You must feel how right it is between us."

She blinked, appeared dazed. Then passion faded, replaced by a regret that worried him. He saw the struggle she thought she hid. Something deep inside this woman was tearing her apart.

"What is it, *querida?* Why do your eyes dim?"

She shook her head, placed unsteady fingers against his chest, then snatched them back as if he'd burned her.

He tipped her chin up, held her in place with just that gentle touch. "Why do you deny us?"

"It's not right." She turned away from him and Joseph could actually taste the frustration in the back of his throat.

"You cannot keep running, Briana. There is something between us…magic, chemistry." *Love.* "Call it what you want, but *something's* there."

Briana whirled around, felt her emotions teeter over that fine line that held the madness at bay, felt reckless words rush forward before she could call them back.

"Yes, there's something there! A baby!" Her hand streaked down to cover her abdomen. Distraught, stunned by her own outburst, seriously considering that she was half insane, she watched the myriad emotions play over Joseph's face.

"Say something," she begged, praying, yet unsure what she prayed for. A hole, perhaps, to swallow her. A pair of comforting arms around her, an assurance that everything would work out all right.

He did an admirable job of composing himself.

"We have made love, yes, but it is much too soon to confirm a conception."

Briana shook her head. "I knew it. You're looking at me like I'm crazy. And to be honest, half the time *I* think I'm going crazy."

"Then you are not attempting to tell me it is my baby?"

"I wouldn't do that." She felt wimpy tears back up in her throat.

His eyes narrowed. "I understood there was no man in your life."

"There isn't."

The pendulum on the mantel clock ticked like a time bomb in the uneasy silence that followed. Joseph's gaze never left her face. "I am confused, Briana. Who is the father?"

Frustration twisted her insides. "I don't know!"

That stopped him for a moment. "How is that possible?"

She made an effort to control her voice this time, to calm her screaming nerves, to brazen past the shame. "I don't know."

Joseph raked a hand through his hair. He couldn't stand to see the tortured look on her face, to see the emotions twist her into knots. He'd known something terrible was bothering her, but he'd never dreamed it would be that she was pregnant. Jealousy pumped through his blood with every beat of his pulse. The idea of Briana with another man made him crazy.

"Let us take this from the top. You say you are...pregnant."

She nodded.

"Yet you do not remember, uh, doing the act that causes this condition."

"Exactly."

The relief in her eyes told him she appreciated his ability to grasp the bizarre series of events. He didn't dare tell her he was in as much turmoil as she. He didn't understand it at all. But he couldn't bring himself to extinguish that light of hope. He would have to tread with caution. The situation was odd, but not insurmountable.

"These things don't just happen," he said carefully.

"Well, *there's* a news flash." Although testy, her tone held a note of hysteria. "I must have blacked out or something. I don't know. I just don't *remember!*"

"Could you perhaps have suffered a trauma?" he asked, still grasping for a shred of coherence in the midst of his confusion.

"I haven't had any that I recall." Briana threw up her hands and nearly knocked over a vase of roses. "Which doesn't mean a whole lot. I just told you I haven't had sex that I recall, either." She paused, met his gaze, couldn't quite hold it. "Other than the night with you."

Joseph had to strain to hear her. But he did. And just that simply, her soft words brought back his focus, cooled his jealousy, reminded him that he would go to any lengths to have this woman, to protect her, stand by her—love her.

"Ah, *querida,* and what a night it was."

"Joseph, please..."

"I am not willing to give you up, Briana." Now

that the initial shock had worn off, he felt more balanced. "No matter what your circumstances are. We will get past it."

"How? I obviously slept with somebody and have no memory of doing it. How do we get past that?"

"With love."

She blinked. He made her want to believe, gave her hope when she'd thought there was none. Still... "This isn't your problem."

"What if I wish to make it mine?"

"Then you'd be a rare man among men. Who are you, Joseph?" she whispered.

"I am a prince."

Briana's jaw went slack for the space of two heartbeats, then she laughed, surprising herself and Joseph, too, if the look on his face was any indication. An unexplained baby was crazy. His rhetorical answer fit somehow.

"*I* know you're a prince, but isn't that a little immodest of you to say so?"

He frowned, clearly puzzled. "No. Not immodest. It is the truth. I am Joseph Lorenzo Castillo. Crown prince of Valldoria and heir to the throne."

## Chapter Six

"You're joking, right?"

"I am not accustomed to joking about my heritage or title."

Her heart started to pound. There was a subtle arrogance in his tone, an air of command in the way he held himself. An image of him at the ball flashed in her mind. Like pushing the Rewind button on a tape player, she recalled the odd way guests had seemed to wait for an invitation to approach him, how they'd treated him with a sort of deference.

"How the heck did you get to be a prince?"

"I was born that way. Firstborn."

"No." She shook her head, feeling the madness return, stronger than before. This was too much for one lifetime. "I'm having a nightmare. Any minute now, I'll wake up."

"I assure you, I am no nightmare."

She still couldn't assimilate it all. "You can't be a prince. Look how you're dressed!" She punctuated the ridiculous statement by glaring at his dirty white sneakers.

He merely shrugged and shoved his hands into the

pockets of his aged jeans. How he managed that, she wasn't sure; the denim fit him like a glove.

"I am not at the palace, nor do I have duties pressing today. Even royalty are allowed casual days."

"Royalty..." She covered her face with her hands. Oh, dear Lord, she didn't know which emotion to feel, didn't know whether to be embarrassed or horrified. How dared he not tell her this!

"If you're a prince, how come the media wasn't all over you at the benefit?"

"It was not known that I would be there. My decision to attend was last-minute."

"Okay. One night you gave them the slip. But I know how these things work, Joseph. Why aren't the paparazzi hiding in my bushes?"

"Because my people have deliberately leaked the information that I am in the States. Besides, I am not so newsworthy as you might think. We are only a small country. I generally keep a low profile and am not so hounded by headline seekers as a more well-known prince would be."

His explanation didn't ease her turmoil. It only made it worse. She had an idea he was downplaying his celebrity status, and all sorts of horrifying thoughts sped through her mind. One thing was for sure, though. The man wasn't joking.

"Criminy! I slept with a prince!"

His brow arched. "Yes."

"A *prince!*"

"I believe that has been covered."

She poked him in the chest. "Don't you patronize me."

"I wouldn't dream of it."

She studied him, checked for hidden sarcasm. "Good, because I'm royally pissed at you."

"Pun intended?"

She blinked. "No, it was not intended. But I like it. Yes. Absolutely. I'm *royally* pissed."

"I am glad we got that straight."

His voice was a little too smooth, way too calm to suit her roiling emotions. She felt like screaming, didn't know which way to turn, and paced instead. "What made you think you could keep something like that to yourself?"

"The subject did not come up."

She stopped, whirled around. "The subject didn't..." Her breath hissed out. "Oh, just shut up and let me think."

Joseph felt his hairline shift as his brows rose. After his astonishment at being told to shut up had passed, he had to bite his lip to keep from grinning like a fool. He had an idea she might actually strike him if he gave in to the incredible surge of joy and laughter he was feeling right now. She was something to watch—all righteous indignation, pacing like a sleek cat in a cage, her fertile mind obviously working overtime, curly autumn hair swishing across her shoulders with her agitated movements.

He relaxed his stance, prepared to enjoy the show. She didn't disappoint him. As he'd expected, the fireworks erupted again.

"I don't believe this. I don't know who the hell I slept with to get pregnant. I'm dealing with a memory blip and a baby conception that I can't explain. As if that's not nerve-racking enough, I've added another glitch to the insanity and slept with a prince!"

"I think I might object to being called a glitch,"
he injected, then shrugged when she just ignored him
and continued to pace, picking up throw pillows and
tossing them back down. Tension screamed from
every action, and yet when she touched a bloom on
any of the various flowers in the vases, her fingers
were gentle.

He was charmed.

"How could you dupe me this way? Not tell me?"
She didn't wait for an answer. "There I was, imagining myself as Cinderella at the ball, dancing with
the handsome prince. And dear God, you *were* a
prince."

Smart man that he was, he refrained from agreeing.

"And you let me take you to that simple restaurant—sat at a picnic bench when you're probably
used to dining tables that seat twenty."

"Thirty-five, at least."

"And you ate *pigs'* balls."

"Now that did shock my royal sensibilities."

She glared at him—no, it was more like she was
looking right through him. A novel experience, to say
the least.

"And then there was the night we spent together!
Oh, I could just scream. Or slug you." She plowed
her fingers through her hair, wreaking havoc on the
disarrayed curls. Suddenly, she froze in mid-step and
slapped a hand over her eyes. "Dear heaven, do
princes actually make love like that?"

Joseph nearly choked. Obviously, in her tirade,
she'd forgotten for a moment that he was in the room.
Her head whipped around, curls bouncing, her

green eyes narrowed. She poked him in the chest again, causing him to take a step back.

"Damn it. I heard that."

"What?"

"That choking noise. Are you laughing at me?" She punctuated the question with another jab.

"I wouldn't dream of it." He gently grabbed her finger and held it against his heart, utterly beguiled. This woman yelled at him, cursed him, even. No one in his life had ever had the nerve to do so. He'd always been waited on, bowed to and revered. He'd been surrounded by people since birth, yet he'd been sad and lonely.

Briana made him feel alive.

He felt her hand tremble against his chest, saw the moment she gathered her control, realized what she'd said and to whom she'd said it. Shock registered in her wide green eyes. Amusement followed, as he'd known it would.

Her lips curved and laughter spilled out, infusing the air with a joy that was nearly tangible.

"I'm hollering at a prince!" She rested her head against his chest, tried to gain composure, then went off into another peal of laughter. "Please tell me that's not a capital offense or something."

Joseph grinned. "Under the circumstances, I am inclined to grant you leniency."

She thumped him in the chest.

"You doubt I have the power to grant a pardon?"

"I'll take the fifth on that. For all I know, doubting a prince is cause for beheading."

"Ah, no, *querida.* I assure you we are a civilized

country. And such a pretty head...it would be a shame to detach it."

"Flattery won't cut it this time. You have some explaining to do, *Prince* Joseph. But I need to sit down. The shock appears to be affecting my knees."

She backed away and sat on the couch. He started to join her there.

"Uh-uh." She shook her head and pointed to the chair opposite.

He shrugged and changed directions, easing himself into the chair facing her.

"So, tell me. What were you really doing in Monte Carlo and why did you hide your identity?"

"Attending the same benefit you were, and I wasn't hiding anything."

"Omission, then."

"Do we want to debate omissions?"

*Absolutely not.* "You're stalling. The benefit was two weeks ago. Why are you still here?"

"Because you are."

She closed her eyes, that wily little thing called hope doing its darnedest to sidetrack her. "You don't have any...uh, *prince* work to do?"

"Not for the next few weeks. I have given myself a month's vacation of sorts—of which two weeks has already slipped by," he added archly.

Briana frowned, wondered if she was affronted, decided to ask before jumping to conclusions as she normally did. "You're not by any chance blaming me for half your vacation being squandered, are you?"

"I did not say 'squandered.' I said 'slipped by.' There's a difference."

He didn't really answer the question, but she decided to let it go for now. "You mentioned you were looking for a woman...." A statement that had given her a bad moment or two.

"Yes. I was betrothed to—"

She gasped and shot straight up off the sofa. "You're *engaged?* Criminy, Joseph, if there are any other slight bombshells you need to drop, please do it now. I'm about at my quota for shocks."

"I am not the only one dropping bombshells," he reminded. "And please sit, *querida.* Your pacing makes me dizzy."

She sat automatically, realized what she'd done and almost sprang back up. "Do you call all your subjects that?"

"You are not a subject. And no. Only the woman I am in love with."

She wondered if he could see her heart beating in her mouth. Her tongue felt thick, her vocal cords shaky. "I wish you wouldn't say things like that."

"It is the truth."

"Maybe you're just infatuated."

"No."

She was afraid of that. Especially because she felt the same. However, being in love with Joseph, the man, was entirely different than—

"Lordy, a prince. I can't get used to it. I feel..." At a loss, she paused. "Do I bow? Kiss your hand? What?"

A spark of annoyance flashed in his eyes. "No."

"Don't people usually?"

"Yes. Usually."

"But you don't like it."

"It gets a little tiresome."

"I can imagine." She rolled her eyes. "What am I saying? Of course I can't imagine. You were going to tell me about the fiancée."

"Arranged marriage," he corrected. "And this conversation is wearing me out. Could we stick to one subject at a time?"

"We could try. But I've got to tell you, my mind's racing. When's the wedding?"

He shook his head, obviously switching conversational gears again. "To Raquel?"

"Is that her name? It's pretty."

"Yes. And to answer your *question,* on the *subject,*" he punctuated the words with a considerable amount of control "—there isn't going to be a wedding."

"Did you cry off?"

"That's an old-fashioned term. And yes, in a manner of speaking, I called it off by simply not making it official."

"Can you do that?" She slapped a palm to her forehead. "Oh, I keep forgetting. You're a prince. So, naturally you can do what you want."

He uncrossed his legs, leaned forward and rested his elbows on his knees. "Briana?"

"What?"

"There is no need for this subject hopping and false joviality. You are attempting to avoid the real issue."

She closed her eyes and took a deep breath. She might have known he would see past her nerves. "The main issue is mine alone to bear, Joseph."

"It doesn't have to be."

"How can you say that? Especially now?"

"Why especially now?"

"Because you're a prince."

"We've covered that subject. Thoroughly. I am a powerful man, Briana. And that power can go a long way toward righting wrongs—or uncertainties, in your case."

"What are you saying?"

He reached out and took her hands in his. "Marry me, *querida.*"

Shock held her silent for several heartbeats. Then she jerked her hands back, scooted farther into the couch, away from his touch, away from her own crazy impulse to leap into his lap. "Are you out of your mind?"

"No. The last time I checked, I was quite sane."

"Well, check again. You might come up with a different answer. For all I know, my insanity is catching."

"Don't."

She closed her eyes, shook her head.

"I warned you before, I had intentions of marriage," he said softly.

"That was before."

"The baby revelation?"

"And the prince thing."

"That 'prince thing' isn't so bad. You would love my country," he said, his voice gentle. "We have a metropolitan center, yet there are miles and miles of open country, with beautiful vegetation, clean lakes and beaches...waterfalls emptying into serene grottos."

Briana was intrigued. He knew just which buttons to push, knew she loved adventure, dreamed of exploring new places. She shouldn't ask, but couldn't seem to stop herself. "I suppose you live in an obscenely large palace?"

He chuckled. "Obscenely. The structure alone covers seven acres."

"Just the house? Good heavens, who cleans it?"

"I have no idea."

"That's awful."

His brows rose and she laughed. "Oh, dear, I've insulted the prince again. That just goes to show there's no hope for me."

"There is always hope. And you do not insult me—just take me by surprise on occasion."

"So, how many rooms are in this castle?"

He shrugged. "I stopped counting at two hundred. And before you pass judgment on my person again, I would challenge you to try and keep track."

"I imagine it could be done."

"Who would want to?"

"Beats me. I'm having trouble just getting my imagination to picture something so grand. Tell me more."

"Size-wise?"

"Sure, go ahead and brag." She closed her eyes and settled back against the cushions.

"Let me see. The grand hall alone covers twenty-eight hundred square feet. Just getting to the front door is a workout in itself."

"Hmm," she mumbled. "A woman could drop fifteen pounds in nothing flat."

"Ah, no, *querida,* that would not be good for the baby."

She stiffened, made a conscious effort to relax. "You're taking me out of the fantasy. Keep talking."

"The *palacio* was built back in the 1600s, as a fortress against enemies. Since that is no longer a concern, the grounds have been redesigned for pleasure to the eye. Grassy slopes move in sinuous curves down to the lake, where there is a charming boathouse guarded by stately oaks."

She popped open one eye. "Do you have a boat? Besides the cruise-ship yacht you've got out here in the harbor?" she clarified.

"Several."

"Figures."

"Our country's leading industry is platinum. I am a very rich man, Briana."

She sat up, alerted by his tone that the verbal tour was over, which was a pity. He painted beautiful pictures with his softly accented words. "Your point being?"

"You and the child you are carrying will want for nothing."

His gaze rested on her stomach with such a gentle, possessive look, she could have wept. "You're offering me the fairy tale, Joseph, but it just won't work. You're royalty. I'm just a girl from Ohio with a degree in languages and a yen for travel."

"It will work if you will stop being so pigheaded and just let it be."

"One of us has got to be realistic. Besides, your family's bound to give us opposition."

"My family will love you. And we will claim the baby is mine and no one will be the wiser."

Everything within her stilled. She tried to imagine

what it would be like if this child were actually his, and found herself wishing with all her heart that it was so. "Could you do that?"

"Yes." His tone was resolute, leaving no doubt as to his sincerity. "The child is part of you, therefore easy to love."

A prince, she thought. In more ways than one. He made it all sound so simple when it wasn't. "You're forgetting a small detail, here. I haven't got a clue about this child's paternity. There's no telling what he or she will look like."

"What's your point?"

"Your features are very distinct, Joseph. You said so yourself that your lineage is impeccable. I'm not about to be the one who messes that up."

"Let me worry about what's going to be messed up."

"It's not just me," she said softly. "I've got a child to think about now. An innocent baby who deserves to fit in, no matter where we end up. You're nobility—"

"You've said that already. Do you think that means I cannot be a good father?"

"No. You would make a wonderful father. You're one of the rare men who can accept and give love. But what about your peers? Your family? The people of your country who you'll one day rule? The people who will expect your heirs to be their future leaders? What if I *did* marry you and for some reason we were unable to have more children?"

"You're borrowing trouble where there is no need."

"Okay. What if we had more kids? *They* would be

legitimate heirs. What would that say to *this* child?'' She placed her hand over her womb. ''That he or she is not good enough?''

''*Por Dios,* Briana. These difficulties will not arise.''

''Can you guarantee it?''

''Yes, damn it. I am the prince!''

She gave him a bittersweet smile. ''All the arrogance in the world won't sway the minds of citizens brought up with tradition. You're something of a celebrity, I imagine—even though you claim otherwise. Tabloids and historians will dissect your life, write about it, hold it up for public speculation. Your royal commands won't prevent that.''

''Want to bet?''

''It wouldn't be fair to take your money that way.''

''What I have is yours, Briana.''

''I'm touchy about that sort of thing, Joseph—being a kept woman and all. I've always made my own way in life.''

''You would not be a kept woman.'' He wanted to shout the words, shake this woman. How could he convince her that they were right for one another? Duty and honor were important to him, yes, as was his family. But Briana Duvaulle moved him. She was the woman he'd been searching for all his life, and he just hadn't known it.

In two short weeks she'd turned his world upside down and her resistance was tearing him up. He didn't know how to get through to her, didn't think he would survive if he couldn't. No longer could he imagine a future without Briana in it.

Frustration twisted inside him. Didn't this beautiful, obstinate woman realize that people were supposed to capitulate to a prince's wishes?

The instant the thought surfaced, he felt a twinge of disgust with himself. That kind of thinking was just what had started this life-altering two weeks, beginning with Raquel. Exactly what he'd chafed against, what he'd found unacceptable in his life—in the woman who had been chosen for him at birth.

After thirty years of tradition, he was no longer satisfied with the way people went along with his wishes, could no longer accept the idea of spending his life with a woman who'd been trained to live her life through him.

Two weeks ago, at a betrothal ceremony, that custom had suddenly appeared barbaric to him, a custom that his ancestors before him had embraced, but one he'd realized was intolerable for himself.

He wanted a woman who had opinions and goals and dreams of her own.

Well, Briana certainly had all three. And he didn't want to take her unique opinions away from her. He just wanted them to be the same as his. He suppressed the nagging voice that told him he was operating on a mental double standard.

It wasn't as if he was asking her to give up something important to her, he rationalized. He was offering her the moon and the stars if she wanted them. Offering to move heaven and earth for her happiness.

*Por Dios.* He could afford anything she could possibly hope to want.

Yet the stubborn woman didn't seem to care about his money and position. No, she was concerned about *him,* worried that he might be making a sacrifice.

She obviously did not understand the full impact of what it meant to be a crown prince. He would see to it that no child of his was ever slighted. In that respect, title and power would come in handy. In his world, it was possible to *command* acceptance.

The problem was, he didn't want to command Briana. He wanted her to come to him of her own free will.

And he wasn't above hedging his bets.

He rose, pulled her to her feet and caught her chin in his hand to hold her still. He noted the astonishment in her green eyes an instant before his lips took possession of hers. She tasted of raspberries and silk and heat. He felt her automatic response, yet he didn't allow himself to linger. If he did, he would never have the strength to step back, which he finally did with a great deal of reluctance.

He saw the pulse beating wildly at her throat, the dazed look of passion in her eyes.

"You can hide behind all the words and excuses you want, *querida,* but you cannot hide from this. We were meant to be, sweet Briana. You will see."

She obviously did not understand that full impact of what it meant to be Joseph's partner. He would see to it that she did. If she was overwhelmed, it but capped his and polished anticipation in finally, in this world, in using available...

*Chapter Seven*

The doorbell rang at 6:00 a.m. Groaning, shoving hair out of her face, Briana stumbled from the bed. "Somebody better be dead or have a damned good excuse why they're not," she muttered and yanked open the door.

It took her a second to realize it was Joseph. Her brows drew together. "If you're not here to tell me you're terminal, I'll take care of it myself."

He brushed a kiss on her lips. "Good morning to you, too." He moved past her, circled the room and inspected the blossoms on the flowers—which were still perky. A lot more perky than she was.

Briana sighed and barely controlled the impulse to slam the door. The scent of his cologne filled her nostrils, clung to her lips. "Do you know what time it is?"

"Ah, you are not a morning person, I see. It is these small details that we must find out about one another. Not that I doubt our compatibility, you understand."

Her brain was definitely sluggish. Still, she had enough cells working to level a comeback. "How can you form *any* opinion about our compatibility? To borrow your words, we've made a habit of intimacies before niceties.''

His sensual grin made her rethink her intelligence and her degree of alertness. She'd obviously overestimated both and had played right into his hands.

''We must remedy that, I think.''

''Could we do it at a more decent hour?'' She checked the clock. ''On second thought, it'll have to wait. I've got a busy day ahead of me. Is there a point to this visit?''

''Breakfast.''

Her stomach revolted. Unconsciously, she placed a hand at her abdomen. ''I don't think so.''

''Morning sickness?'' He was at her side in three steps, his hand covering hers, his brown eyes concerned.

Although he wasn't actually touching her belly, she could feel the warmth like a scorching desert sun—a heat that sent shock waves through her body. She stepped back. ''I don't eat breakfast.''

''Then you must start. You have another life to think of now.''

''Joseph—'' The doorbell pealed again. Her breath hissed out. ''I am seriously considering getting violent, here. Has everybody forgotten how to tell time?''

''Perhaps you should allow me to answer that.''

''It's my house.'' She snatched open the door and stared. A waiter in a crisp blue uniform stood staring back. She realized then that she was entertaining uninvited guests in her shorty nightgown.

Joseph eased up beside her, put himself between

her and the bemused waiter. "You may set up in the kitchen, I think," he said to the man. "The lady is not dressed for patio dining."

"Well," Briana said. "Since everybody has seen…everything, I suppose I'll go put on some clothes. And the patio will be fine, thank you." Joseph might be used to princely dictating, but she wasn't in the mood. In fact she was feeling downright surly—a common occurrence when she didn't get enough sleep.

And she would lay those sins right on Prince Joseph's doorstep, she thought as she yanked a ratty sweatshirt over her nightgown. If he expected her to dress for the occasion, he could think again.

That parting kiss he'd given her yesterday had been meant to shake her up, to show her what she would be missing if she continued to hold him at arm's length. Well, it had done the job—in spades—and kept her tossing and turning all night, had her entertaining all sorts of rationalizations.

Rationalizations she simply could not allow herself to indulge in.

Breakfast, she thought. Delivered to the door. Who else but a prince would do something like that? Normal people ate at restaurants or cooked for themselves. It just went to show how far out of her realm Joseph Castillo really was.

If words wouldn't get through to the thickheaded man, she would have to show him by actions that she wasn't suitable to be a princess.

She caught her reflection in the mirror, paused, then picked up a brush and ran it through her hair. Imagine, she thought, a princess…

"Oh, for Pete's sake." She slammed the brush down and went out on the patio. The waiter and his metal cart were gone. The glass-topped table shaded by an umbrella was laden with fragrant rolls, jams, and two steaming silver pots.

Joseph glanced at her, and raised a brow. "Nice sweatshirt. Goes with the gown." He poured a cup of tea and handed it to her. "I figured you'd prefer something light. Continental cuisine rather than heavy sauces."

She eyed the coffeepot the way an alcoholic might fixate on a tumbler of whiskey. Resigned, she sipped the healthier brew.

"Sit," he said. "Enjoy."

"This bossy side of you is wearing thin, Your Highness."

"Ah, and here I thought I was charming you."

She sat and eyed the array of food set out before her. Maybe she was hungry, after all. "I refuse to be charmed," she muttered.

"Of course not," he said affably. "Tell me about these busy plans you have for the day."

"Job hunting."

He shook his head and tsked. "Waste of time."

"Why?"

"You will only have to quit soon."

"I've got awhile before the baby comes."

"I wasn't referring to the baby."

She paused with the cup halfway to her lips. "What, then?"

"When we are married, there will be no need for you to work. Unless you want to, of course."

"Joseph—"

"With all the travel we will be doing, it could become a problem. Reliability and all that. By all means, though, you should do what pleases you."

Her eyes narrowed. "You're not playing fair." He knew just how to get to her, knew that the lure of travel would poke holes in her resistance.

"There is an American saying I am sure you are familiar with. All's fair in love and war."

"We're not at war."

"No. We are in love."

Her insides jolted. "Maybe you are."

"I will remember this penchant for testiness in the early mornings."

"Do that." And she would remember the power of his devastating smile.

He chose a fluffy croissant, took his time buttering it. "You are determined to obtain a job?"

"Yes."

"What are your prospects?"

"I have an offer at a flower shop."

"Strawberry or raspberry?"

"Excuse me?"

"Jam." He held the butter knife poised over the glass containers.

"Oh. Raspberry."

"Just as I thought. And your qualifications for such a position?"

It took her a minute to recall what they were talking about. Her brain kept getting snagged on the shape of his hands, the way he cupped the warm roll in his palm. "It's a fairly straightforward job."

"If it is a flower shop you are wanting, I'll buy it for you."

"Would you stop saying stuff like that? It's not normal."

He shrugged. "It is for me."

"Well, it makes me a nervous wreck. I don't want to own the shop. I just want a job." She didn't know whether to laugh or scream. "And as for my qualifications, I minored in horticulture."

"I might have known that—based on the abundance of greenery in your home."

"To which you've added."

"See? It is fate that I instinctively knew your preferences." He made another pass over the croissant with the jelly and laid the knife across the china plate.

"Don't act too smug. There aren't many women who don't enjoy pretty flowers."

"But you enjoy them more than most. Do not burst my bubble. We are making progress."

She smiled, and couldn't stop the gurgle of laughter. "You're incorrigible."

"Yes. Now you are catching the spirit."

"What spirit?"

"The exchange of information, the getting-to-know-you process. You have discerned that I am incorrigible and I did not even have to tell you so. Here, eat one of these croissants while they are still warm."

He held the bread to her lips, caught a trickle of butter with his thumb as it dribbled down her chin. She watched as he licked his thumb, found it nearly impossible to swallow.

"Juice?" he offered.

She could barely tear her gaze away from him. It seemed that even his simplest movement created images of sensuality. Her own tongue made a sweep over lips slick with sweet butter and raspberries.

His Adam's apple bobbed in a slow swallow. "I could have done that for you," he said, his voice sandpaper rough.

"Thanks just the same." She took a gulp of the pulpy juice—fresh-squeezed, she noted, surprised her brain was capable of assimilating any sort of impression. Lord, if he kept looking at her like that she would surely melt into a puddle right here on the back courtyard pavers.

"How much time do we have?"

She nearly choked. "Not *that* much."

He threw back his head and laughed, startling a pair of doves resting on the stucco patio wall. "Sweet Briana, where is your mind?"

"Certainly not on the same wavelength as yours." *Liar.* She plucked at her sweatshirt, which had suddenly become entirely too warm.

"Did you think I was referring to making love?"

"Don't try to tell me you weren't. I saw that come-and-get-me-baby look in your eyes."

He grinned, tried to look shocked. "I am sure I do not possess such a look. It would not be proper for a man such as I."

"Don't pull that royal-highness stuff on me. If your eyes were any hotter they'd spark."

He chuckled. "That is one of the things I enjoy about you, Briana. You are very frank. And we can if you want to."

"What?"

"Make love."

Her heart nearly pounded out of her chest. "Just

because I let you buy me breakfast doesn't mean I'm easy." It seemed she was destined to embarrass herself this morning. She would be more careful what connotations she put on his words. "What was the time reference for?"

"Our getting-to-know-you process."

"I have a job interview. We can't cover all that in an hour."

"Ah, you have at last answered my question. An hour will be a good start. My favorite color is green. Your turn."

She stared at him blankly. She'd thought the sexual innuendos had woken her up.

Obviously she was mistaken.

"The color you are most partial to," he coached.

"Oh. Peach, I guess."

"See? Something else we have in common."

She frowned. "Did you spike your orange juice? You said green."

"Yes, but I adore peach. Reminds me of your skin."

She rolled her eyes. "Okay, I get it now. Music. I like rock and roll, loud and throbbing with base."

"Saxophone," he returned. "Rhythm and blues, moody." His brows arched. "Close enough to be compatible, don't you agree?"

Yes, she adored jazz, too, but she wasn't about to tell him so. She was feeling a touch ornery. "Has that monstrous-size palace ever had rock and roll blaring in its hallways?"

"As a matter of fact, I believe Antonio has done so on occasion."

"Antonio?"

"My younger brother. He likes to call himself the black sheep of the family...or the spare, because he is the second born."

"Does he resent you?"

"Not at all. Antonio courts danger in any form—from fast cars to fast women. Royal duties would cramp his style."

"Yet they don't cramp yours?"

He took his time answering, his expression pensive. "At times, perhaps."

Undercurrents of their impasse stirred heavily in the silence that followed his admission. There was simply no way to come to terms with the fact that she was pregnant with heaven-only-knew-whose baby and that condition could very well destroy his reputation and the fabric of an entire country.

She looked away, unable to bear the longing for something she couldn't allow herself to have. "I've got to get ready."

"Is a job really necessary?"

"Yes." She knew how to stand alone, how to take care of herself. It had never been this hard before, though.

"Very well. I will not hold you up." He stood and brushed a soft kiss on her lips. "Leave the dishes. Someone will be by to pick them up."

"I could get spoiled." She hadn't meant to voice the thought, and knew he would jump on it.

"You deserve to be spoiled."

"My mother might disagree. She claims it's an ugly trait, inspires laziness."

"Your mother is an entire ocean away."

"True."

"And I do not believe it is possible for you to possess ugly traits." He reached out and tucked a strand of hair behind her ear, a gesture that was somehow more intimate than a kiss, a gesture that nearly brought tears to her eyes. "Good luck on your interview, Briana."

"Thanks." She wanted to ask when she would see him again but didn't. She had decisions to make about a job and her future.

And as much as she longed for it to be, consorting with a prince was not on the list or in the cards for her future.

PERHAPS THE REASON she loved the little town of Antibes was because of its lively ambience that didn't rely on tourism to keep it afloat. The narrow, bustling streets were a joy to traverse, evoking both a sense of adventure and serenity in Briana.

She knew most of the shop owners by name, asked after their children and elderly folks, and never tired of strolling through the produce market in the cobbled *cours Masséna,* the main street of the old town.

As luck would have it, Marie Saincene was expecting a child any day now and pounced on Briana's inquiry about a job.

"Oh, you are a saint," Marie said, her swollen stomach lightly bumping the worktable strewn with flowers. She was a petite woman with tiny feet. Briana should have hated her on principle alone. Instead, she felt an immediate bonding with the sunny-natured florist—a response that was becoming a habit.

"I have been putting off advertising for assistants because I am so territorial about this shop. But Marcello is insisting, and I must admit I am becoming tired.''

"I can imagine."

Maria laughed. "Oh, do not worry. I am not about to pop—although Marcello watches me as though I might.''

Briana couldn't keep her gaze from straying to the apron straining over Maria's protruding stomach. Something fluttered inside her, and for once, she could actually imagine herself at such a stage.

The problem was, the image playing through her mind was of Joseph—of his gentle, bronze-skinned hands resting possessively over her stomach, his fingertips lightly touching her as he soothed away her aches and pains, his brown eyes shining with the joy he shared over their child....

She shook her head, silently admonishing herself for the flight of fancy.

Wishing wouldn't change the paternity of the tiny life growing inside her.

"How much time will you be taking off?" she asked.

"Only a few weeks, if all goes well."

Briana hedged, remembering Joseph's reminder of reliability. Her life was so up in the air, she couldn't guarantee where she would be ten minutes from now. And to that end, she needed to be honest.

"I'm not certain how much time I'll be able to give you. I'm not a permanent resident of Antibes, and, well, I'm going through some difficulties of my own right now.''

"Expecting a child, no?"

Briana sucked in a breath as panic jolted through

her with a swiftness that left her dizzy. She felt exposed, heard a roaring in her ears and wondered if she was about to faint. She grabbed the wooden worktable for support. How had this woman known her secret? Had somebody been spreading rumors? A man, perhaps, whom she couldn't remember? The thought sent a wave of shame rushing through her.

"Are you unwell?" Maria rushed forward and laid a concerned hand on Briana's arm.

"I'm fine."

"Breathe deep and it will soon pass."

She did, the heady fragrance of roses and carnations reaching out to her like a lifeline.

"Better now?" Maria asked.

Briana nodded, although her insides still quaked. She'd probably blown her chances for the job, and although she was terrified to ask the question screaming in her mind, not knowing was an even worse prospect. "How did you know?" she whispered. "About the baby?"

"Oh, it is quite obvious. There is a glow unlike any other when a woman carries a child in her womb. Even if she has not accepted such a miracle, the bloom cannot be mistaken. It is like with the roses, when they begin as tight buds and soon relax into the soft inevitability of an open, unique blossom."

"That's beautiful," Briana said, steadier now that she knew Maria's knowledge hadn't come from vicious rumor. She glanced once more at the straining girth beneath Maria's apron. "Are you scared?"

"About the birth?"

"Yes. And the changes it will bring. The responsibility. The uncertainty."

Maria smiled gently and stroked her hands over her stomach where her child rested. "Naturally, I am a tiny bit frightened. I am a worrier over the smallest detail—this shop, the competition in a village such as this where flowers are grown in abundance. I am fearful of missing opportunities and I work like a madwoman to press ahead. Yet I have Marcello, who keeps my feet on the soil. He can look at me at the end of a day, smile his special smile, and I know that all will be fine. He is the perfect balance for my stubborn independence and neurotic inclinations."

"I could write a book about neurosis," Briana said dryly. "You're very lucky that you have a great husband."

"Yes. Is your child's father not that special man in your life?"

Briana looked away, shook her head. She thought of Joseph again, how *he* might have been that special man if the timing had been a little different, how she longed for him to be the one she could turn to at the end of a busy day. But acting on that longing would have great consequences for him, no matter how strenuously he denied it. He was in the public eye—a royal prince. Even if she allowed him to claim this child as his own, some nasty tabloid would ferret out the truth.

For all she knew, the real father of her baby would recognize her and come forth trying to cash in on Joseph's fortune. It upset her that there was a possibility she'd slept with someone who might be lower than pond scum.

And it made her crazy that she just couldn't remember.

Her reaction to Maria's intuitive guess was a lesson in reality that had become murky with Joseph's attentiveness. She would have to make a greater effort not to forget that lesson.

Maria touched a hand to Briana's shoulder, bringing her out of her musing.

"Let me show you your duties."

"You mean you're still willing to hire me?"

"Oh, yes. Although I suspect you are much too qualified for the position, my beautiful flowers will be in good hands with you. Whatever hours you are comfortable working, or for how long is your choice. Marcello has promised to bring in his family to help in my absence. Do not fret that you will put me in a bad position if your life takes an unexpected turn."

THE SAME DELIVERY BOY who'd worn a path to her doorway for the past two weeks was camped out on Briana's front step when she got home. He'd been paid to wait, he said, and when she opened the jeweler's box, she understood why.

Nestled against a backdrop of black velvet was the most exquisite necklace she'd ever seen. Set in platinum, the stones were brilliant. It wasn't extravagantly large and gaudy, but neither were the gems small. Tasteful, striking, exactly the sort of piece she would have chosen if she could afford it.

Sparkling prisms sprayed the room like a kaleidoscope when she shifted the box to extract the card tucked beneath the clasp.

Emeralds for the color of your eyes, diamonds for the sparkle of your happy laughter. Trust me.
                                                        Love, Joseph

A lump formed in her throat. Flowers and breakfast she could accept in halfway good conscience. A necklace that had probably cost more than she would ever make in a lifetime was a different matter.

Not daring to try it on, she closed the lid. Like the equivalent of Cinderella's glass slipper, she was terrified it would be a perfect fit.

And that she would never find the courage to give it back.

Oh, how did she ever get in such a mess?

When the phone rang, she considered not answering. She didn't want to talk to Joseph until she'd found some backbone. And when she found it, she intended to go to him, on his own turf—or boat, rather—and put a stop to things before she was in so deep that her heart would never recover.

Which, if she were honest, was already too late.

The phone continued to shrill. Calling herself a coward and a wimp, she lifted the receiver.

"Hey, toots, how's life?"

"Dad." Her fingers relaxed and her heart softened. Closing her eyes, she could picture Thomas Duvaulle sitting in his wheelchair, an atlas spread open before him. She sank down on the settee by the phone, suddenly wishing there wasn't an entire ocean separating them.

For the first time in a long while, she wanted to just curl up on her father's lap and pour her heart out the way she'd done as a child.

But she couldn't. She couldn't tell him about the baby or Joseph or of losing her job at the consulate. Not yet, anyway. He was counting on her to live his dream of traveling the globe, a dream that had been shattered by a fall and the confines of a wheelchair. Dear Lord, she had let him down; she'd messed up in a really big way.

Tears gathered in her throat, stung her eyes.

"Bri? You okay, toots?"

She sniffed. "I'm fine, Dad. A little homesick, I guess."

"Now I know something's wrong. Are you crying?"

She forced a laugh. "Of course not. Just a cold I picked up. Even high-class parties aren't germ free."

"Been to some good ones lately?"

"Well," she hedged, teasing. "Would you consider a charity benefit in Monte Carlo where a girl can rub elbows with movie stars and a bona fide prince a good one?" She felt a piercing in her heart and ignored it.

"Sounds pretty decent to me." He chuckled at the understatement. "A prince, huh?"

"Yeah," she said softly. "A Latin prince."

"And how does one go about gaining entrance to such a party?"

"One has a cousin whose fiancé moves in such circles." As she'd done so many times, she embellished the story with far more details than one might impart when describing an evening out. She made sure he could taste the meltingly tender grenadins of veal, hear the haunting strains of the orchestra's violas, see the glitter of glamorous gowns worn by the wives of the elite.

He was especially intrigued that she'd actually met

a prince, so she played it up, leading him to believe her information had been gleaned over a polite cocktail. With her hand gripping the telephone receiver, she painted a picture for her father of a palace that sat on three hundred acres—almost the size of Monaco itself—of opulence and yachts and enormous grand halls.

And never once did she give away that on that magical evening, she'd fallen in love with the handsome, incredibly tender, Latin prince.

# Chapter Eight

"Permission to come aboard, Your Royal Highness. Unless, of course, you are entertaining a *bella*. In which case, I will make myself scarce."

Joseph shook his head and grinned at the sight of his brother standing on the dock. He wanted to be annoyed at the intrusion, but he couldn't. Not with Antonio.

"I'm not entertaining at the moment."

"More's the pity," Antonio said, boarding the ship, glancing around with the eye of a man who adores sailing.

"What brings you here, Tony? It is not Grand Prix season, nor are there any regattas to compete in."

"Do I need a reason to visit my favorite brother?"

"As a rule, yes. And I am wise to that innocent look you are wearing."

"You always were the smarter son. I have been sent by the queen to straighten you out."

"I was not aware that I needed straightening out."

"Ah, you have perhaps forgotten a certain heiress to whom you are betrothed."

"Was."

"Not according to Mother."

Joseph stared out over the harbor as a beautiful sloop motored out of the marina, causing the rigs moored nearby to bob gently. "I will phone her."

"Cold, Joseph." Antonio tsked. "Very cold."

"I meant Mother, not Raquel."

"Not a smart idea. Nothing short of your presence will calm that particular storm."

"I'm not ready to return yet, Tony."

Antonio gave a long-suffering sigh. "I was afraid of that. Actually, I have an ulterior motive for being here. You have given Max and Pedro the slip, which leaves you unprotected. What if someone were to take a potshot at you? Then I'd have to take your place, and I most assuredly do not wish to be in that position."

Joseph laughed. "Have you taken up fiction reading while I was not looking? There is no danger of people taking potshots at me." Valldoria was a peaceful country where the economy flourished due to the abundance of platinum. In his opinion, there was little need for all the security. Besides, he was tired of everyone fawning over him.

"Well, it seemed like a good excuse. *Dios,* Joseph, it is unseemly for a crown prince to go about unescorted."

"I do not want an escort. Especially now."

"Ah, yes. The famous courtship we have been hearing about." Antonio grinned. "You may have sent your bodyguards home, but Mother sent them right back. As we speak, Max is probably holed up on the yacht in the next berth."

Joseph raised his voice, making sure it carried over

the water. "Maximilianus is employed by me. Not the queen. If he is still anywhere on the Riviera, I will personally fire him and make sure he does not find future employment as a bodyguard—on any continent." Sure enough, the curtains on the adjacent boat fluttered.

Joseph deliberately turned his back and grinned. After a moment, he asked, "Is he leaving yet?"

Tony's lips turned up, his playboy smile full of teasing and genuine affection. The two shared a rare closeness, free of any competition or jealousy. "Give him a minute. He's just tripped over his bag."

"Dangerous thing for a man his size," Joseph commented idly. "He'll probably fall in the water, then one of us will have to go in after him."

"Don't look at me. These are eight-hundred-dollar shoes."

"I'd expect you to take them off if you were to go swimming."

"Why don't you go swimming?"

"Because I'm the crown prince. And what the hell are we talking about, anyway? Max is lethally trained and would not be so ungraceful as to fall in the bay. Is he gone yet?"

"Yes."

"Good. When you get back to Valldoria, make sure everyone knows that I will not stand for spies."

"Including me?"

"You, I will make an exception for. You're not one to carry tales back to the parents. Besides, you are easy to blackmail. Have you forgotten the incident with Mother's orchid garden?"

"Careful, my prince. Blackmail can be a double-edged sword. Have you forgotten your part in the episode? Knowledge and omission would be considered abetting. Besides, I am not so worried. Mother is a romantic at heart. She would no doubt approve of me impressing a *bella* with a yacht fragrant with rare orchids."

"Care to test that approval, little brother?"

"I will pass, thanks. I have never been a tattletale. Besides, I am on Mother's persona-non-grata list for missing your betrothal ceremony, and you are now making my atoning process quite difficult."

Joseph grinned. "She must have been some woman for you to risk Mother's wrath."

Antonio shook his head in mock sadness. "Why will no one believe that I simply missed my flight?"

"Probably because I happen to know you were piloting your own flight."

"*That* qualifies as grounds for blackmail. So, in light of my zippered mouth, you must tell me what I have missed and why you have taken leave of your senses. Why one beautiful, perfect woman is not enough for you."

"You are speaking of Raquel Santiago?"

"She *is* your betrothed."

"Was. And granted, she is beautiful, but she is far from perfect."

Tony's jaw dropped. "She has been groomed to serve as your future queen, Joseph. She will cater to your every whim. Any man's fantasy, I would think."

"That's barbaric," Joseph said in disgust.

Antonio, rarely at a loss for words, paused. "Did somebody knock you in the head, or what? I was not aware that you felt this way when I left."

"Neither was I."

"And you are sure that Raquel will not suit you?"

"*Por Dios,* Tony, I have only laid eyes on the woman twice. And both times, she was afraid to speak to me."

Antonio stared in astonishment for another moment. "Are we talking about the same heiress, here?"

"You mean she talks to you?"

"Sure."

Joseph frowned. "Then it must just be me."

"Well, you can be kind of stuffy and intimidating."

"Briana does not appear to be intimidated."

"I wondered when you'd get around to her."

Joseph turned and put his hands on the deck railing, his gaze tracking a gull as it skimmed the surface of the aquamarine water.

"She is unlike anyone I have met, Tony. She makes me feel alive, when I was seriously doubting that I had any emotions inside me to begin with. She's not impressed by my title, she'll yell and curse at me and put me in my place even when I don't realize I need putting there. Her laugh lights up a room, she's beautiful...she stimulates me."

"Cursing and yelling will have that effect."

Joseph's eyes narrowed.

"So what's the problem? Why do you not just bring home the happy woman, break Raquel's heart and be done with it?"

"Melodrama does not suit you, Tony. And since you have had conversations with my former betrothed, you must know that her heart is not involved. She has no more feelings for me than I do for her.

As for Briana, she has a misguided notion about her lineage not being up to my standards."

"Could she have a point?"

Joseph looked at his brother. "Tony, if you fell in love—fell hard—would a woman's background make any difference to you?"

"I am not about to fall in love, so the question is not one I can answer with authority. I am also not in your position, Joseph," Tony said quietly, seriously. "There are certain expectations that go along with your title."

"That's just it. It shouldn't be that way. I want more. Duty shouldn't come with such a high price tag. It shouldn't mean that a man should sacrifice his happiness. Stretch your imagination, Tony. What would you do?"

Tony shrugged. "Court her, I suppose. But we are still comparing apples to oranges. Since you are the heir and I am just the spare, it is much easier for me to run away from home."

Joseph shared his brother's grin. "Is there talk at home that I have run away?"

"Yes. And it is unseemly for a man such as you."

Joseph laughed, long and hard, and clapped Tony on the shoulder, causing his brother to stare, first in astonishment, then with approval and camaraderie.

"I am having an excellent time being unseemly."

Tony nodded. "Then I will leave you to it—unless, of course, you need some pointers from an expert."

"This is a solo flight," Joseph said. "I'll wing it."

"In other words, get lost? Say no more. I have, after all, fulfilled my obligation to Mother. And there is a certain actress on location in the Florida Keys who I have promised to wine and dine.'' Tony moved toward the gangway, then paused and looked back. ''Just be careful, *mi hermano.* I'd hate to see you crash and burn.''

BRIANA WONDERED IF SHE could find his yacht among all the fancy ones bobbing in the famous Monte Carlo marina. There was some major money tied up in these pleasure crafts.

She gathered her bearings, located the balcony they'd stood on just two short weeks ago and focused her gaze toward the tip of Nice.

The *Royal Valldoria* stood out like a swan among newborn ducks. *Figures,* she thought. She should have just looked for the biggest one out here.

A yacht befitting a prince.

Late-afternoon breezes fluttered her skirt against her calves and toyed with her hair. She shoved the curls out of her face as she navigated the floating dock.

He stood on the deck, watching her approach. Dressed casually in white shorts, a knit shirt and deck shoes, he was the picture of the idle rich. Except she knew he wasn't idle. He was a prince, facing responsibility for an entire country.

A prince on vacation who seemed determined to bring home a princess.

But Briana was no princess.

Sadness and longing nearly overwhelmed her. For an instant she resented the child growing inside her with a fierceness that brought immediate shame.

But resentment wouldn't get her anywhere. She'd always taken responsibility for her actions. Even though, in this case, she couldn't remember the circumstances.

Only the consequences.

"Hi," she called softly. His skin was the color of someone who'd spent hours in the sun, a rich hue contrasted by the white of his shorts. Sensual lips curved into a tender, welcoming smile, highlighting the slash of high cheekbones and boyish dimples.

With a casual swipe at the dark hair that perpetually flopped over his forehead, he held out a hand to assist her aboard the boat.

The minute his palm engulfed hers, Briana was lost. Why was it that it only took a mere touch from this man to turn her knees and emotions to jelly? To throw her carefully laid plans and words into chaos? To send her straight into rationalizations? Just a few minutes more, she would promise herself. An hour. A day. Just one more day, she thought. What could it hurt?

"I'm glad you came," he said. "I've wanted to show you the boat."

"Cruise ship," she corrected with a smile.

"It was built for entertaining. I must admit, I enjoy the space."

"Do you skipper it?"

"I have. Most of the time I leave that for the crew, though."

She glanced around at the inviting lounge chairs resting on the polished teak deck. Her flats were soft-soled; still, she wondered if she should remove them. She decided that wasn't necessary when she noticed Joseph's leather slip-on's—worn without socks. For an instant, her imagination snagged on those muscular, well-formed legs; how they'd felt sliding against hers....

"Would you like a look?"

Her eyes snapped up to his. "A look?" Her face flamed when his lips turned up in a knowing smile. She'd been looking plenty and had been caught.

"At the *Royal Valldoria.*"

"Sure." She might as well build another memory to relate to her father. Once she returned the necklace there would be no need to ever see Joseph again.

It took more than an hour to complete the tour. Inside, rich teak and mahogany shone like mirrors. Plush carpet, the color of melted platinum, stretched across floors and hallways. The sofas were a deep wine silk with the Valldoria crest woven into the fabric. A Steinway piano sat in the corner on a dance floor. The drapes were pure silk in the same subtle pattern as the furniture. Teak slat blinds mounted inside the window frames guarded against the sun.

Joseph watched the awe on Briana's face as he led her through the various staterooms aboard the yacht. He realized he'd gotten into a habit of looking straight through his possessions. They were just things, and rarely did he look closely, or take time to appreciate their beauty.

He'd never known poverty, or even life as a middle-class citizen. For thirty years, he'd been surrounded by riches and opulence—and people just like himself, who accepted the trappings of wealth as commonplace.

Briana's joy and wonder when she reverently ran her fingers over a malachite vase, smiled at his mother's collection of pomanders, or drew in her breath at an original Picasso hanging over the wet bar made him experience the appreciation through her eyes.

But if the way she clutched her purse was any indication, the lady did not intend to stay.

"This is...very grand," she said.

"I'm glad you like it. Would you excuse me for a moment?"

She nodded and watched him leave the room. Or did they call them rooms on boats? When he didn't come back right away, Briana became antsy. The necklace was still in her purse, and her fingers were getting a cramp from holding the bag so tightly. She relaxed her grip, figuring the jewels were safe enough here. A thief probably wouldn't be interested in the bauble once they got a look at all the other stuff on board.

She heard something creak, felt herself sway slightly and reached for the piano to steady herself, then immediately snatched her hand back when she realized she'd made fingerprints on the glossy surface. Checking to see that nobody was looking, she used the elbow of her sweater to wipe away the evidence.

"I bet there're no kids allowed on this ship," she said, then jumped and whirled around guiltily at the sound of Joseph's chuckle.

"Actually, Antonio and I were practically raised on yachts very much like this one."

"You're kidding." She gave another surreptitious glance at the piano—at the smudge still there. "Did they have priceless paintings and pottery sitting around, or did your mom have the good sense to kid-proof the area?"

"My mother encouraged learning and exploring. Whether you're three or thirty, she invites you to touch and enjoy her treasures. The appreciative touch of hands and the feast of eyes gives objects their character, she says."

"Expensive character if it falls on the floor."

"My mother believes that nothing is irreplaceable—except human life."

"Some mother," she said in wonder.

"Yes. Some queen."

Reality slammed into her with the force of a charging bull. "Oh, criminy, Joseph! Your mother is the queen!"

He laughed. "And a very good one."

"But she's your *mother*."

"The queen's title impresses you, yet mine does not." He shook his head, amusement dancing in his dark eyes. "You are tough on a man's ego." Gently, he touched a springy curl, brushed it back off her shoulder. "Shall we go up on deck?"

"Sure." When he looked at her like that, touched her that way, she lost the ability to think, much less breathe. With his hand at her waist, he guided her up the stairs.

The first thing Briana noticed was that the scenery had shifted. For a minute she thought they'd come up a different set of stairs.

"Joseph? We're moving." No wonder she'd felt woozy.

"Yes."

"But, we can't. I hadn't planned to stay."

"I know. That is why we are no longer stationary."

Her heart pumped in both dread and anticipation. "In the States, we call this kidnapping."

"It could be considered as such on the Riviera, too." His shoulders lifted in dismissal.

She arched a brow. "I doubt that even a prince is above criminal charges."

"If one were to press those charges, perhaps not," he said softly. "Will you charge me with the crime of loving you, *querida?*"

Her heart lurched right up into her throat. "I wish you wouldn't say things like that."

"Why? Because it makes you want to say it back?"

"No," she lied.

His palms cupped her cheeks, his fingers gently smoothing tendrils of hair from her face as the breeze whipped it forward. "I am having a party aboard the *Royal Valldoria* tonight. Will you join me?"

She cleared her throat and tested her voice, which sounded odd in her ringing ears. "Where are the guests?"

"I am looking at her."

She closed her eyes, nearly groaned at the invitation in his softly accented voice.

"A private party, Briana. Say yes…live a little. You know you want to…listen to the water slap against the hull, dream of far away places."

"I can hardly say no. We're already under way."

"Ah, but it is your choice. I can have my *capitán* turn around."

She shook her head, stepped away and leaned against the rail. The sensuous beauty of the ocean at sunset was too much to resist. Any moment now, the sun would set fire to the smooth face of the sea. And she had an excellent vantage point from which to watch the spectacular sight.

And excellent company.

Instead of feeling trapped, she felt free. She was exactly where she wanted to be, even if she *shouldn't* want it. Rationalizations again, she thought. Joseph was in the driver's seat, sweeping her away on a journey. She had a choice, but he made it so easy for her to forget, to deny for just a little while longer.

He made it so easy for her to dream.

"I've been promising myself I'd take a sunset cruise."

"And now you have your wish."

She looked at him, automatically reached out to brush back the hair that flopped over his forehead, watched as the breeze whipped it forward again. "You're good at that."

"What?"

"Granting wishes...giving gifts." She undid the clasp of her purse and removed the velvet box. "The necklace is beautiful."

"I'm glad you like it."

"I can't keep it." She held the box out.

"Why not?"

"It's too expensive."

"I assure you, it did not even make a ripple in my bank account."

"You can brag all you want, but I'd be scared to death to wear it. I— What are you doing?"

He took the box from her fingers, unclasped the hook of the necklace and stepped behind her. "You must model it for me."

"No." She reached up, felt the cool stones against her fingertips, told herself she was only touching them to ensure they didn't fall if he lost his hold on the delicate clasp. "I told you, I can't—"

"There." He pressed his lips to her neck, rearranged her hair over her shoulders and turned her so he could get a better look at the fiery gems. *"Magnifico."*

Heat radiated at her neck. With trembling fingers, she stroked the emerald and diamond facets, reveled in the delicate weight against her collarbone as the platinum backing slid against her sensitized skin.

"Now you've done it," she moaned. Just as she'd expected, it was a perfect fit—if a necklace could be described as "fitting." But to Briana, that was how it felt. Now it would be next to impossible to give the gorgeous stones back.

"Done what?"

"Never mind. It's a Cinderella thing. You wouldn't get it."

"You wound me, *querida.* The fairy tale is required reading for a prince-in-training. However, I am not certain I understand the correlation between a glass slipper and emeralds."

"Did I say anything about a glass slipper?" Was the man a mind reader? And if there was such a thing as a course in princely behavior, he would have aced it.

He grinned. "I will buy you those, too, if you wish."

"That's just it. You've got to stop *buying* me things."

"But I take great pleasure in it."

She heard the tinkle of fine china and glanced around. Like a silent elf, somebody had set up a table for two, complete with white linen and crystal. Candles protected by cut glass glowed softly against a backdrop of the Riviera shoreline.

"Oh, Joseph," she whispered. "You're a hard man to resist."

"That is what I am counting on." He held out a chair, waiting patiently until she sat.

"So where is this dinner cruise headed?"

"Just along the coastline. I have secured mooring at the port of Antibes."

"For how long?"

"As long as it takes."

It was both a warning and a promise. Candlelight danced over his features, accenting his prominent cheekbones. She tore her gaze away, shifted to the side as a waiter placed a chilled salad plate in front of her. Why didn't she have the backbone to stop this before she got in even deeper? His expressions and actions spoke so much louder than words. He didn't intend to let up on the courtship, and he was moving closer in order to conduct it.

Everything he did or said impressed the heck out of her, weakening her resolve.

"How did you know I would come here tonight?"

"I didn't."

"But the meal…"

"The staff aboard the *Royal Valldoria* is always prepared for guests."

"Figures."

"Is the luxury so difficult for you to get used to?" She didn't answer. If she voiced the yearning, it would only make it more real, so much harder to dismiss. She finished her salad, sipped iced mineral water, and gazed out at the Côte d'Azur as the sky darkened.

During the day, the sea was a mass of pedal boats, bobbing bodies, Jet Skis and sailboards. Now, the sensuous blue Mediterranean took on the reflection of lights from grand seafront hotels and lighted marinas.

The *Royal Valldoria* cut through the calm waters with little effort, lulling her into a dream state of luxury that, yes, she would love to get used to. Lights carpeted the hillsides like swarms of fireflies. Headlights from cars stuck in traffic jams on the Corniche roads seemed another world away. Here, on the deck of a multimillion-dollar boat, the bustle of everyday life gave way to fantasy.

A fantasy that she could hold in her heart and someday take out and examine, relive, tell her child about.

Pain threatened to swamp her. Would she ever tell her child that he or she had had the opportunity to have a prince for a father? An opportunity she couldn't allow herself to accept, for herself or the child.

Would a child understand that she couldn't accept the dream at Joseph's expense? That she couldn't be the downfall of a special, tender prince?

Another woman might choose differently. But Briana couldn't. Honesty and honor were too deeply ingrained in her.

"You know, you're leaving yourself wide open, here, Joseph. You can't just go around picking up women and telling them you're a prince and lavishing expensive gifts and dinner cruises on them.'' *Or offering to be the father of their baby.* ''You run the risk of having someone fall for you because of your money.''

''I don't make a habit of conducting courtships this way. Only with you.''

Oh, the fairy tale was getting so bright it almost blinded her. Honor was definitely overrated. ''So, how do you know *I'm* not after your money and title?''

''Because you fell in love with me before you knew of either.''

''I did not fall in love.''

He talked right over her denial. ''And you have done nothing but give me grief over my title.''

''There is that.'' She took a bite of salmon, closed her eyes as the tender fish melted in her mouth. ''My compliments to your chef.''

''He will appreciate it. And the two of you have much in common.''

''I doubt it. I'm only a generic cook at best, and I have a habit of burning stuff. This salmon is better than any I've tasted.''

He smiled. ''I was referring to attitude. He, too, sneers at my title. Touchy man, but worth his weight in platinum.''

''I don't sneer.''

''But you are not impressed.''

''Well, that's not exactly true. I might be a little impressed, but I wouldn't want it to go to your head or anything.''

He chuckled. ''I should have invited Antonio to stick around. He would have approved of you.''

"Your brother was here?"

"Mmm. Apparently the family thinks that turning thirty has affected my mind."

"That's usually a woman thing," she said offhand. "Did you do something to upset them? Forget a ribbon-cutting ceremony or something?"

"No. Apparently I did not make the severing of my betrothal clear."

Briana's hand stilled against the icy glass of water. By rights, another woman should be sitting here, enjoying the sea air and elaborate candlelight dinner.

"Joseph, women are kind of funny about relationships and how they end. If a woman is planning a wedding, she wouldn't take it very well if she weren't absolutely certain whether or not she had a groom who'd show up."

"Raquel will not care one way or the other. She has been brought up differently than a girl from the States."

"But surely you have broken her heart. Oh, I feel just awful." He wasn't hers to hold, but if he were, she wouldn't want to share.

"Don't. I have not broken her heart. She did not have feelings for me—at least, feelings that were her own. She has been told since birth that I was her destiny. She had little choice."

"And you don't think altering that direction all of a sudden will throw her into a tizzy? I've got to tell you, if it was me, I'd hunt you down. And I would be armed."

"I would like to count on that."

"What—that I'd shoot you?"

"No. That you'd care enough to come after me."

There was a trap here, a trap she desperately wanted to put her foot in, but knew she shouldn't. Trying for nonchalance, she shrugged. "I was speaking hypothetically."

"Were you?"

The intensity in his dark eyes made her look away. "Maybe someday I'll meet your Raquel."

"She's not mine...and you probably will. Her family members are regulars at the palace."

"As if I'll be visiting there anytime soon."

"You will."

She shook her head, felt the dinner she'd just eaten churn in her stomach. "I no more belong at a palace than I belong on the moon."

"I'd take you there, too, if it were within my power."

The absolute sincerity in his soft voice turned the churning into a cauldron of white-hot pain.

"Joseph, don't do this to me. I came to return the necklace and you prolonged my stay by pulling up anchor. Sooner or later, we'll have to dock. And I'll be going my own way."

"Why?"

"Because. There's a piece of my memory that's still missing, and some very real consequences because of it. The puzzle is giving me nightmares and if I have any hope of hanging on to my sanity, I've got to find those answers."

# Chapter Nine

Joseph studied her for several moments. She was running from something and it was more than an unexplained conception—although that was pretty bizarre in itself. She was never idle, constantly moving, on the go, as if ghosts were lurking around each corner.

The impression surfaced at odd times, yet he wondered if he could be wrong. How could someone laugh so deeply, feel so much, enjoy so greatly, if there were heavy things on her mind, in her past?

"Perhaps I can help you find those answers," he said.

Her forehead furrowed. "How?"

"Let me think on it. I am curious, though, why you are so adamant that you will not fit in at the palace."

"Joseph—"

"Aside from the baby," he said, desperate to change the subject. Little by little she was slipping away, and he felt helpless to prevent it. If he could just understand her reservations, he could counter them. "Tell me of your upbringing."

"You mean are there any skeletons in our family closet?"

"No. That was not my meaning. And if there were, it would not matter to me."

"It should." She leaned back as Miguel cleared away the rest of the dishes from their meal. "Okay. Let's see if I can synopsize twenty-six years—" She stopped, pinned him with a direct look that made him want to grin. He loved the way her mind leaped from one subject to the next. "I just thought of something. You mentioned turning thirty. When was that?"

"My birthday was the day we met." In more ways than one, he thought, because on that day he'd felt as if he'd been reborn and had embarked on his true life course.

"Oh, you should have said something. What does a prince get for his birthday?"

"The woman of his dreams."

She knocked over her water glass, closed her eyes, and groaned. Joseph calmly placed a linen napkin over the drenched tablecloth.

"*That* is one of the reasons I wouldn't fit in at your palace. I have decent manners, but I can be clumsy."

He knocked over his own water glass.

Briana laughed. "Oh, Joseph, I'd accuse you of being naive if you weren't a prince."

"Don't let that stop you," he said dryly. "It hasn't so far."

She laughed harder, used her own napkin to blot up the new mishap—this one deliberate. "See. I'd probably insult you in front of the wrong person. Or, God forbid, I'd put my foot in my mouth in the presence of the queen."

"You are borrowing trouble again where there is no need. And my mother will be charmed with you."

"That's debatable."

"We have gotten off the subject," he reminded, still trying to head off her objections.

"Life synopsis. Let's see, I've told you I have two sisters and a brother. Pam's twenty-one, in college. Brock's eighteen and he's just joined the air force. Laura's sixteen, a junior in high school. I was born and raised in the same house in Ohio."

"More common ground," he inserted, feeling smug. "I, too, was born and raised in the same house."

She rolled her eyes. "That's about as far from 'common' as you can get. Our house had ten rooms, total. Yours has over two hundred."

"Minor detail. Where is your optimism?"

"Grounded in reality, where yours obviously isn't. Are you sure you're a prince?"

"Positive."

"Well, I'm definitely not princess material."

"I do not mean to sound pompous, but I have superior knowledge on that particular subject."

"From a skewed viewpoint. My family is comfortable financially, but we're a far cry from rich. I've worked since I was sixteen, as have my sisters and brother. My parents took care of the necessities, but we were responsible for extras, like car insurance, gasoline, and partying."

"You doubt that I have worked?"

"Jobs befitting a prince, maybe." She toyed with her wet napkin and folded it at precise angles. "Joseph, I've done everything from delivering pizzas to working as a receptionist in a beauty salon. I drove a limo once, mostly for kids at high-school proms—

although I did pick up Julia Roberts from the airport, which was pretty cool. I've had boring clerical jobs, sold perfume in department stores, and been a car hop at a fifties diner.''

"A car hop?''

"A waitress on roller skates at a fast-food joint. You know, burgers and malts?''

"I am aware of fast food.''

"But not of servers on skates, which just goes to show how different we are. I can see the headlines now—Prince Cavorts on Riviera with Burger Queen.''

He shook his head, ignored her negativism and gave her a look so tender she nearly slipped under the table. "I do love your sense of humor, Briana.''

"That wasn't a joke. If the tabloids catch up with you—and they will—they'll dig up everything about me and twist it into an embarrassment for you.''

"You could never embarrass me.''

"Then you've got a thicker hide than I do.''

He reached for her hands and removed the damp napkin that now sported permanent creases. "I would never allow anyone to hurt you, *querida*. And I do not believe that you have such a low opinion of yourself. I think you are pulling excuses out of thin air.''

Damn it, the man saw too much. She wasn't concerned about herself. She was concerned over Joseph's reputation. His life.

Women were supposed to talk men *into* love. She never realized how frustrating it could be to try and talk one *out* of it—for his own good. "What makes you think I'm grasping for excuses?''

"Your eyes give you away.''

She sighed, pulled her hands back and looked out at the dark sea. "That's what my dad always says."

"The professor, right? The one who indulged your dreams of travel."

"Yes."

"Does he share your wanderlust?"

"Through books and videos. He's in a wheelchair."

Joseph felt the undercurrents again, saw shadows chase the light from her expressive green eyes, knew somehow she hadn't meant to impart that piece of information. "Did he suffer an accident?"

Briana's gaze was unfocused as she stared at the winking lights of another pleasure ship farther out to sea.

"He fell from a ladder...getting a book down for me." Her breath felt trapped in her throat, aching, suffocating. The horrible scene scrolled through her mind in sickening slow motion—a nightmare she would remember for the rest of her life; a nightmare she still cried over when no one was around to see.

"He was busy with paperwork that day, but he stopped to indulge my curiosity when I asked him where Fiji was." She gave a derisive laugh. "Fiji, can you believe it? I'd read about it in a book—I don't even remember what book it was. But I was intrigued, thought it sounded romantic. I wanted to see a picture."

She shoved her hair back off her forehead, tried to block the vision of her father lying in a crumpled heap on the library floor. "I should have climbed the ladder myself."

"You are harboring guilt that his accident was your fault?"

"He wanted to travel, Joseph. The kids are almost grown. He'll be retiring soon. He and Mom should be looking forward to spending their golden years in freedom. He gave up so much for us kids. Now...I try to make it up to him, try to make my experiences and memories his."

"I believe your father would tell you your guilt is misplaced."

"Yes, he would. That doesn't mean I don't still feel it."

"Is surgery an option?"

She shook her head. "His spinal cord was damaged."

"A wheelchair does not mean he cannot experience travel, Briana. People do it all the time."

"I know." Her voice trembled with the effort to hold back tears. She hadn't admitted these feelings to another soul; hadn't meant to. Now the flow of words wouldn't stop, ripped out from some painful place deep inside her.

"But he'll never ski down a mountain, or scuba dive in the Caribbean, or walk through the dappled serenity of an Amazon rain forest...."

This time, he didn't give her a chance to back away. He scooped her up, cradled her on his lap. "And neither will you, you are thinking? Because of the baby?"

She held herself rigid in his arms, shrugged instead of answering, hated herself for thinking selfish thoughts, for feeling resentment, for feeling so mixed-up.

Hated herself for wanting something so bad—for wanting to turn back the clock, to be able to call Joseph her own—knowing she couldn't lay claim to either desire.

"Briana, having a child is only the beginning of a new dream."

"It's just so hard to accept. If only I knew for sure... You can't imagine what it's like. This void. The shame of not knowing what I did."

He rested his palm over her stomach.

She stiffened. "Don't."

"There is no place for shame between us, *querida*. This is *our* child growing in your womb."

Oh, if only that were so. She felt so confused, so damned tired. He battered her resistance with only the gentle sincerity of his words. Before she could call it back, hope took wing in her chest.

She turned, buried her face in his neck, inhaled the scent of his cologne. His arms held her in comfort, yet the heat of his body pressed so tightly against her was anything but soothing. She felt the rigid outline of his arousal beneath her thighs and felt her own response tingle in every mixed-up nerve ending she possessed.

Every time she looked at this man, her heart lurched. All she could think about, remember, was their incredible night together; the absolute rightness she felt whenever she saw him, touched him, imagined him.

Selfishly, she wished the world would stop on its axis, wished it was possible for a moment in time to simply freeze, wanted desperately to pretend that only she and Joseph existed in a realm where there were no unexplained babies or class distinctions or possibilities of insanity at the ripe old age of twenty-six.

His utter acceptance of her chipped away at her resolve. This man was almost too good to be true. Perhaps she was deluding herself, but her feelings were too powerful to resist, and Briana found that she was weak after all.

Soon enough he, too, would see that tender words were comforting, but unrealistic. Joseph believed that love could move mountains.

Briana knew that it couldn't. She had plenty of guilt over the ruination of her father's life. She wouldn't add to the guilt by ruining Joseph's.

She felt his lips at her temple, the sweep of his palm against her back. Duty would call him home soon. But until then... Until then, she could pretend. Resisting him, resisting what might have been, was simply too much.

"You never showed me your bedroom when we toured earlier," she whispered.

He went utterly still. "No. I did not want you to think I was rushing you or expecting more than you wanted to give."

She cupped her palm against his face, prayed that she could find her voice, prayed even harder that she could let him go when the time came. "Could you...could you go ahead and rush me?"

Silence hung heavy in the salty sea air. A gull squawked. Wood creaked as the ship yawed over an unexpected wave.

"Are you sure?" he asked at last, his body tense with the effort of maintaining control. Having Briana on his lap, breathing in her unique scent, tested his limits.

"I need you, Joseph."

She might as well have added, Only for tonight. Joseph read the thought in her eyes. But he didn't care. Her admitting that she needed him was closer to an admission of love than he'd gotten so far. He would take it.

She wound her arms around his neck as he stood and carried her below. "You're the only man who's ever carried me. I'm so big."

"Hush. You fit perfectly in my arms."

He elbowed aside the canopy netting, balanced a knee on the firm mattress and pressed her against the silk spread, urgency making his movements rougher than he would have intended. Her lips were pliant and welcoming, her auburn curls like silken threads where they crushed against his pillow.

His mind had been torturing him with images of her vibrant body for two weeks now and it was all he could do to keep from yanking her skirt up and taking her right then.

But he wanted more—her surrender. Totally. Every nerve in his body was on edge as he cautioned himself to take it slow. Yet, everywhere his gaze touched threatened that control—the curve of her jaw and cheek, the shape of her mouth, the outline of her breasts that strained against the lightweight sweater.

She reached up with trembling fingers to touch his face. And in that moment he was lost. She was his only need, his only quest, his only hunger. His mouth came down on hers again, fast and fevered.

He would not be able to go slow after all, he realized. She tasted smoother than any wine he'd ever drunk; she tasted of seductive raspberries and aching desire and hot sensuality. She tasted of both trembling acceptance and reserve.

That reserve ignited his determination, unleashed the storm. Something dark and frightening whipped through him, consuming him. He needed to banish that hesitancy, to make her his, to convince her—body and soul—that this was right, that *they* were right.

"You have my heart, *querida.*" For an instant, his roving hand stilled against her belly, slipped beneath her sweater, caressed the softly rounded swell of her tummy. His fingers flexed gently, reverently, against her skin.

"You *are* my heart." His words were hoarse, yet he gathered her to him in an embrace that spoke louder than any words, releasing a matching fire in Briana, a need so all-consuming she could barely think.

Her breath caught in a sob as his hands once again swept a fevered path over her body. She clung to him, helpless to do anything less, her mouth seeking his, feeling the wild beat of his heart against hers.

This was a different side of Joseph—a side that was both thrilling and frightening. She rolled with him across the bed, frantically tugging at his shirt as he swept her sweater and skirt from her body.

In Spanish, he whispered words of praise against her lips, her throat, and the curve of her hip, his voice raspy. Her own answering murmurs made little sense. Desire spiraled straight to the top, skipping all the stages in between. She couldn't grasp a single thought for more than an instant. She just wanted him to hurry; to appease the desperate ache that flowed inside her like molten lava.

By the time they were naked, her skin was slick with perspiration, as was his. Greedily, her hands roved over his shoulders, his muscled back, his buttocks. Her skin was alive with awareness, tingled at the slightest brush of his fingertips, the sensations humming through her like a rain of falling fireworks—hot, bright, stunning. And still, she couldn't get close enough.

She felt a scream of desperation building inside her.

Outside, the sea slapped gently against the hull of the ship, but inside this cabin, there was a storm of beating hearts and fevered touches, frantic whispers of need.

His mouth closed over her breasts, worshiping, wringing a cry of excitement that took her by surprise, took her right to the verge of ecstasy. She couldn't breathe, yet knew she must.

She rolled with him, straddled him, pressed against his shoulders as he reached for her.

"No. Let me." He'd given her so much. Exquisite memories, beautiful words, pleasure so intense she didn't think the sensations would ever dim. Even over a lifetime.

And she wanted to give something back to him.

She wanted to give him words, sincere words, to tell him that she would be all that he needed. But that would be a lie.

She couldn't promise him "forever."

So she promised him her heart and soul, in silence, in spirit, letting her hands and lips speak for her;

poured every bit of the emotion screaming through her into her actions, her intimate kisses.

Joseph's hands fisted against the sheets. Her mouth was sweet, hot velvet. The rasp of her tongue against his belly, his hips, his manhood, nearly sent him over the edge. He felt his control slipping, and tried to call it back. He felt the silk of her hair brush his thigh, noted the contrast of her creamy skin against the darker hue of his own. Proud and naked, except for the emeralds and diamonds at her neck, she simply took his breath away.

That she could give him such pleasure, so honestly, so selflessly, touched him as he'd never been touched before. He wanted to press her to his heart and never let go, wanted to hold her forever.

He wouldn't let her slip away. He'd never kissed a sweeter mouth, never been so swept away by a woman. He was sure he would never survive without her in his life, and was determined to make sure she stayed there.

He'd never believed it was possible to fall so hard, so fast.

Heart pounding, certain he was about to go mad, he pulled her up his body, rolled with her, parted her legs with his knee. Her eyes were closed, her cheeks and throat flushed with desire.

"Look at me, *querida*."

Her eyes opened, bright green, liquid with a vulnerability that passion couldn't hide. The scent of raspberries and desire hung heavy in the air. And in that instant, he knew she would promise him anything. But would the promise still hold true in the morning?

Slowly, inch by inch, he filled her, his eyes never leaving hers. He felt his manhood swell, welcomed by her feminine warmth, and pressed deeper still until she said his name, her voice hitching on a sigh.

The sound unleashed his urgency. Joseph lost himself in the heat, the bliss, the surrender she offered with her body, yet held back with the shadows in her eyes.

Her nails dug into his shoulders as he poured every bit of himself into her, hard and fast. He wanted to give her everything, be everything for her—was desperate to show her just that.

He felt the pulsating of her womb, watched as she came apart beneath him, marveled at the exquisite beauty of her unguarded display of emotion. Blood pounded at his temples, roared in his head, yet he gave her more, even as he drove himself mad.

Her eyes widened in surprise as her pleasure peaked, then went higher. Her chest heaved, her breath straining. When she cried out his name again he released the tight rein on his control, felt the rush of incendiary heat speed through his body, and consume him. For an instant he teetered on the brink, then lost all ability to think as he tumbled from what felt like the highest peak of a mountain, free-falling further into love.

SOFT RAYS OF DAWN spilled through the stateroom window. The boat rocked gently, but she could tell they were docked—where, she wasn't sure. She looked around the cabin—something she'd been too preoccupied to do when Joseph had carried her here last night. Rich platinum and burgundy evoked im-

ages of elegance and style. Diaphanous netting can-
opied the four-poster bed and draped in soft folds
around all four sides. The dressing alcove next to the
square porthole held a cozy grouping of furniture—
and was bigger than her entire bedroom at home.

Beside her, heat radiated from Joseph's body. She
closed her eyes, nerves crowding in her throat. Heavens, what a night.

She had to seriously consider her conduct. Why in
the world didn't she have the willpower to stay out
of his bed? Was there some "floozy" flaw in her
character she didn't know about? It certainly had
never surfaced before.

Or had it?

That thought brought reality crashing down around
her—reality she'd been able to ignore while she'd
been cosseted in Joseph's arms.

But making love with him didn't change things;
only stirred a vortex of rushing uncertainty.

She was pregnant with no memory of having done
the deed. Trying to force the recall only made her
heart pound and her insides twist. She had to question
her sanity, her morals—the very fabric of her life.
How had she acted that day? Had her behavior been
so bad, so wanton, so lacking in principles, that her
mind had deliberately blocked the experience, holding
it hostage lest she succumb to the insanity?

Nausea churned in her stomach. Heat flushed her
body—the heat of shame, the shame of the unknown.
Sister Mary Kathryn at Saint Bernadette's would have
a fit.

A groan slipped past her throat. Forget the nuns.
Her *mother* would have a fit.

The bed shifted, the sheets sliding across her naked breasts. She looked at Joseph and found that he was awake. Suddenly timid after what they'd shared in this bed last night, she glanced away.

"You are building walls, I think."

"I didn't come here for this."

"And neither did I intend it. But you must know it was inevitable."

Yes. She did know that. Still, it didn't give her wayward morals the boost they obviously needed.

"What are you worrying over, *querida?*"

"The dark flaws in my character, I guess."

"You must not speak of flaws. You are perfect just as you are."

She pulled the sheet higher, feeling exposed. "Perfect little Catholic girls do not wake up and find themselves inexplicably pregnant."

"Pregnancy is quite explainable."

"Yes, but *who* caused it?" Oh, that sounded terrible. Especially since the man who lay beside her, stark naked, was *not* the sperm donor in question.

"Is it so important?"

"Very." If a wannabe hussy lurked in her personality, she wanted to know about it—or her.

"Then we will re-create the day. Search until we find the answers. Together."

"Why? It's not your problem." And what if the answers they found were too horrible to face? Good Lord, she couldn't guarantee what this baby would look like. For all she knew, the father might be a Martian!

"I do not view it as a problem." The warmth of

his palm seeped into her hip and spread to her abdomen as he stroked her there. "Only you do."

She tried not to tense, fought the melting in her soul that made her want to simply throw caution to the wind and turn to Joseph, let him be her prince on a white steed—just like in the fairy tale. "One of us has got to think logically."

"Very well. Logically, with great attention to detail, we will traverse the streets, retrace the steps you might have taken that day, explore any acquaintance you may have made."

Acquaintance? The turmoil inside her gave way to a bubble of laughter.

"You find my suggestion amusing?"

"No... Yes... I don't know, Joseph. Either I laugh or I might scream my head off. And if I do that, I might never stop."

He gathered her close, and pressed his lips to her temple. "Scream if you want, Briana. I will be here to catch you."

"Will you?"

"Always."

Musical words, yet unrealistic. He would be returning home soon. And she couldn't go with him. But what would be the harm in spending the remaining time with him? He offered to help her find the missing link, to give her burning goal direction when her mind was devoid of coherence, totally lacking a solid plan.

If she could find that missing piece it would be a miracle. And if miracles were possible, maybe, just maybe, there would somehow be hope for her and Joseph.

She sighed, seriously afraid her mind was stuck in la-la land, desperately clinging to the slip of possibility that it was not—that hope might spring eternal, after all.

"I feel like I'm at a dead end, like there's a thick wall there that won't let me pass. And until I break through, everything I am is in question. I'd...I'd like some help."

"But?" he asked, tipping her chin up, holding her gaze. "I hear hesitation in your tone."

"I'm embarrassed," she whispered. "I keep wondering what you must think of me. What *I'll* think of myself if I find the answer and it's not... Oh, Joseph, how could I have done something so irresponsible?" *So totally out of character?*

He kissed her closed eyelids, her cheeks, stroked the hair back from her forehead, uncurled her fisted grip against the sheets.

"I have said it before, *querida.* There is no place for shame between us. What I am thinking of you is that you are the most giving—"

"Obviously," she interrupted with a desperate groan.

"Stop that. You are full of joy and life, unique, without artifice. There is nothing tawdry about your morals, nothing ugly about what *we* have shared together. You are all of my dreams wrapped in a bright bow, and that also includes the child resting in your womb. I do not need answers, but you do, so I will do everything within my power to help you find them. In fact, we will start today."

She almost leaped on his offer. Then she remembered her obligations. This penchant for forgetting things was becoming a habit. "We can't start today. *Some* of us," she stressed, "have to work. What time is it?"

"Six-fifteen." He sat up, started to reach for her and frowned when she scooted away. "What work?"

She swung her legs out of the bed, snatched up her sweater and pulled it over her head. "I got a job at Marie Saincene's flower shop."

"Briana, there is no need for you to obtain employment."

"I've already obtained it."

"Then call and cancel. After last night, I thought—"

"You thought wrong," she interrupted before he could finish the statement. "The only thing last night changes is that I've realized that two heads are better than one and maybe you can help me out with this memory thing. Where are we, anyway?" A glance out the window showed a harbor much like the one they'd left from.

"You are the most stubborn woman...." He located his own pants and pulled them on. "Unless Diego defied my orders and sailed home to Valldoria, we should be at the port of Antibes."

"Looks like he was an obedient captain. I recognize the ramparts and Le Fort Carré." The impressive geometric structure was hard to miss. "Which means I'm close enough to home that I won't have to call a cab."

"That would be unnecessary regardless of our mooring. I have a car waiting."

"Now why doesn't that surprise me?"

"I am slipping, I see. It appears I will need to double my efforts to ensure you are surprised."

She laughed, hooked her skirt at the waist and ran her fingers through her hair, trying to restore some order. "We've had this discussion before about your surprises. Which reminds me." She reached up, and fumbled with the clasp of the necklace.

"Do not attempt to return that, Briana," he warned.

"Or what?" Arms above her head, she fiddled with the fastening, trying to figure out how the darn thing opened.

"I will buy you six more, one for each day of the week."

She gave up on the clasp, and looked at him through narrowed eyes. "You would, wouldn't you?"

"Count on it."

She shook her head, left the necklace where it was—draped softly at her throat. There would be plenty of time to give it back. He would be sticking around for a while, helping her locate her lost mind. And when it was time for him to go, it would be much easier to give back one necklace rather than seven.

# Chapter Ten

"He did what?"

Briana stared at Crystal, then at the car sitting in her driveway. She'd bypassed the waiting limo at the marina in favor of walking, needing the air to clear her head. It was only a short walk.

"Bought the Mercedes for you," Crystal said, beaming as if she herself were the fairy godmother. "It was delivered yesterday."

"He..." At a loss, Briana simply stared at the convertible resting regally by the front door. "He can't do that!"

"Obviously, he did."

"The man has entirely too much money if he goes around buying cars for people."

"Elvis did it."

"Cadillacs, not Mercedes."

Crystal shifted Peppe in her arms and shrugged. "If you prefer a Cadillac, I am sure your Joseph will exchange it."

"I don't prefer—" Her breath hissed out. "What am I going to do with this man?"

"Marry him?"

"Oh, listen to you. The queen of stalling. Franco's been after you for marriage for a year."

"We were speaking of you, not me." Peppe gave a shrill bark to punctuate Crystal's statement.

Briana shook her head, and snatched the keys dangling from Crystal's hand. "I'll just have to return the car."

"Like you did the necklace?" Crystal looked pointedly at the emeralds and diamonds still draped around Briana's neck.

She quelled her automatic instinct to touch the brilliant stones. "I couldn't get the clasp undone."

"And how did it get *done* to begin with?"

Briana looked away, thinking about that floozy gene again, wondering if Crystal might be thinking something similar. "Never mind," she muttered.

"Ah, I see how it is. If I am not mistaken, those are the same clothes you left in yesterday."

The car keys bit into Briana's palm. "Is business off or something?"

"No, the architectural plans are coming along nicely. Why do you ask?"

"Because you seem to have a lot of idle time to spy out the windows and notice what I'm wearing."

Crystal laughed. "There is no need to spy when love is involved. You are like a lighthouse, Bri. Casting off bright signals."

"Love is *not* involved." Was she that transparent? "Besides, he's a prince. Did you know that?"

"*Oui.* I do now."

"Why didn't you say something sooner? Do you know how many times I've insulted that man? Royalty! A prince, for crying out loud?"

"I thought it best that Joseph tell you himself. Besides, I did not recognize him right away. He looks quite different when he is not in the ceremonial dress of his country." Crystal shrugged. "And you know my reading preference leans more toward architectural trends than celebrity buzz. I, most likely, would not recognize Princess Di if she came to the villa and sat down to tea."

"You have a point. Despite your flamboyant look, you're stuffy as all get-out sometimes."

"I see you are not discriminating with your insults. Cousins, princes…but you love us anyway," Crystal added slyly.

"*You*, I love." Briana wasn't about to take the rest of that bait. "And because I love you so much, why don't you take the car?"

Crystal grinned but made no move to accept the keys. "I have my own, thanks. Besides, it is not proper to give away gifts."

Briana ground her teeth. "I've never been proper in my life, and you know it." She dropped the keys in her purse—along with the velvet box that still rested there. An hysterical bubble of laughter welled inside her. One could return a dress to the department store easily enough. Emeralds and a Mercedes were an entirely different matter.

HE FOUND THE FLOWER SHOP in total chaos. Customers stood in line, the phone rang incessantly and cut flowers and ribbons were strewn on every available surface.

Briana was obviously the only one there.

She looked up, waved him in the door, and without a care for his title, pressed him right into service.

"You keep turning up like a bad penny, but in this case, I'm glad of it. Catch that phone, would you? Two lines are holding."

Astonishment snatched his voice for a minute. "A bad penny?"

"A shiny one, then, if that makes you feel better. Now, can you deal with those phones?"

He stared at the blinking buttons as if they were a warning signal for imminent attack. He was used to order. Peace and quiet and calm. And he was used to *giving* commands, not receiving them. "What do I do?"

"Push the button, talk to the person and write down what they want. Wing it." In fluid French, and with considerable charm, she organized the queue of customers, writing sales tickets, swiping magnetic strips on credit cards and pumping helium into balloons.

And the woman claimed she wasn't princess material, Joseph thought. She was a born leader, diplomatic, determined, and unflappable.

A lot calmer than he was. Hell, she made him dizzy just watching her. And he was still staring at the buzzing phone as if it were a venomous snake. Briana appeared to have forgotten about him, obviously figuring he was up to the task based on her sketchy instructions.

Competitive spirit piqued, he punched the red flashing button. The gentleman requested a flower delivery for a woman he'd met on a blind date.

"This date, was it as you'd expected?"

"And then some," the gentleman said, man to man.

Ah, love, Joseph thought, glancing at Briana who worked like a demon, yet made it look effortless. This, he could handle. "Roses, I think. Red ones."

"You think so?"

"I am certain." Feeling like the equivalent of America's "Dear Abby," he offered some parting advice, wrote down the delivery information, then punched the second blinking line. Innate confidence restored, he talked the next caller—an entrepreneur seeking a thank-you gift—into yellow roses, then assured the final caller, a woman wanting to send a birthday gift to a friend, that pink roses were just the thing. If they ran out of roses he would have more flown in himself.

Not too bad, he thought several minutes later, feeling smug. He was starting to get the hang of this salesclerk stuff.

But respite was not on the horizon. A loud crash had him rushing to the rescue of a child who'd tripped over his own shoelaces. The kid survived, the plastic vase filled with baby carnations did not.

The phone pealed again at the same time a woman wearing a fuchsia turban grabbed at his sleeve.

"Young man, I would like to purchase this oncidium."

He glanced at the coral orchid, never slowed his stride. "The dancing lady. Excellent choice. One moment, *s'il vous plaît.*"

Briana caught his eye. "Impressive, Prince."

"My mother grows orchids." He tossed her the orders he'd written, dived for the phone, wiped sweat from his brow and scribbled names and credit-card numbers on new tickets. With the phone cord stretched to its limit, he bumped into Briana twice as they both maneuvered around the scarred wooden counter.

"Young man!" the turban lady insisted, thrusting the oncidium under his nose. Joseph's confidence crumbled like a stale cookie. He wasn't used to juggling this many balls at once.

He decided he'd made a grave error in sending Max and Pedro home. He could have used some assistance. This whole experience was thoroughly out of his realm.

With Briana occupied arranging flowers, it was up to Joseph to handle sales and he suffered a bad moment or two since he didn't have a clue how to open the cash register.

The oncidium woman impatiently clicked scarlet fingernails against the counter. The line of customers waiting to pay grew longer.

Finally, out of desperation, and refusing to look like a total idiot, he took her money, tucked it beside the machine and made change out of his own pocket.

Briana looked over and caught him doing it, but he ignored her raised eyebrow and impudent smile. He had a good mind to tell everybody to pick a flower and take a hike, and then just stuff the cashbox himself. As it was, he made several people's day by rounding prices and giving back too much change.

"What happened in here?" he asked when the phone at last ceased to ring and the crowd thinned out a bit. "Did somebody declare it National Flower Day?"

"I don't know. It's as if the city's gone mad. Hand me that frog."

He glanced around, puzzled, then looked up when she giggled.

"Not *that* kind of frog, Prince. The green thing you stick flowers in."

"Oh. I don't believe I've come in contact with one of those before." He wondered what she would do if he grabbed her and kissed her as his instincts were begging him to do.

"Just shows how your education is lacking… Your Highness." She snipped stems off daisies, poked in some yellow carnations and spoon-tip mums, finishing the arrangement off with a few sprigs of fern.

"I recognized the oncidium, didn't I?"

"True. Fancy flower. Fancy man." Her impish grin took the sting out of the words.

Joseph sighed, wondering how a man got a little credit around this woman, and watched in awe as her capable, artistic hands created beauty out of straggly stems and happy blossoms. And she did it all so effortlessly, with a slight smile on her face and spring in her step. The spring in his own step was flagging, however, and he looked around for a chair.

The "drill sergeant" apparently had other plans for him.

"The little boy who fell, was he okay?"

"Fine. Just wet knees and bruised ego. I dusted off both."

"And did you take care of the mess on the floor?"

"Uh, no."

"Then grab the mop, will you? We'll have a lawsuit on our hands if somebody slips in that water."

Phones and roses, he could handle. Making change was a snap.

Mops were another matter. A man had to take a stand somewhere.

"Briana, I will *pay* for any lawsuits. For that matter, I will pay you triple what you are making in wages to hang up the Closed sign and leave this shop. *Dios,* make it a flat fee. Anything. Name your price."

She gave him a distracted glance, full of chiding and challenge. "Your arrogance is showing, Prince. And you're whining."

His spine went rigid. "I do not whine." Never let it be said that Prince Joseph of Valldoria had backed down from a challenge.

He snatched up the string mop, figuring it couldn't be too difficult to wipe up a floor. Never mind that his mother would keel over in shock and horror if she saw him doing the work of a servant.

And doing a poor job of it, at that.

"Briana, this implement is apparently not functioning properly."

"A mop doesn't function on its own." She pumped helium into yet another balloon, snipped string and tied it off. "*You* make it work. Lord save me from mop virgins," she muttered in German for the benefit of customers still within earshot.

"I heard that," Joseph returned—in German also. "And I still say it is malfunctioning. There is now a wider circle of water smeared than before."

She brushed by him, and patted his cheek. "I have great faith in your resourcefulness. And I like a man who can keep up with me in several different languages."

He shook his head, found himself grinning like a fool and wished like hell the patrons would disappear so he could take her in his arms and kiss that sassy mouth. This was what he'd missed all those years— the spontaneity of conversation, uncensored, and in several languages. No worries over being correct. Just silly and ordinary.

"About that Mercedes..." she said, the next time she breezed past him.

"You were surprised?" he asked, reminding her of their earlier conversation, giving himself a mental pat on the back.

She rolled her eyes and barely spared him a glance as she wrapped a sunflower in cellophane, tying it off with an orange ribbon.

His smugness slipped a notch and the dirty strings of the mop swished to a halt. "You do not like it?"

"I will not drive it," she said, mocking his correct speech. "Everything around here is within walking or biking distance."

"You must have a care for your condition, Briana. Bicycling is definitely out."

"Who died and made you king?"

He made another squiggly swipe with the mop, kept his tone bland. "No one, so far."

Auburn hair swirled across her shoulders. Her eyes widened in horror. "I didn't mean...I forgot about your father—I was joking."

"I know." He chuckled at her stammering repentance. "And you must not worry. The king is in excellent health."

"Still, that sounded insulting."

"No insult taken. As I was saying about bicycling—"

"As I *meant* to say," she interrupted, "there is no danger in doing something your body is used to doing."

"Your nose is growing."

"Excuse me?"

"You did not mean to say that. You *meant* to be difficult."

She laughed, causing several customers to stop and stare. And Joseph was charmed all over again.

"You're right." She wiped her hands down the front of her apron, picked up her cutting shears and called over her shoulder, "You missed a spot to the left."

It frustrated him that she wouldn't slow down, wouldn't give in—that he couldn't *pay* her to drive the car or wear the jewels or quit the job. And wasn't that a kick. He'd left Valldoria, sick of everyone fawning over him, tripping over themselves to grant his every wish.

Well, Briana certainly didn't fawn. Somehow he needed to find a happy medium or his lady would be questioning *his* sanity as well as her own.

In the meantime he still had to finish mopping the damned floor. And while he was at it, he vowed to give the palace maids a raise at his first opportunity.

"Where is your help?" he finally asked during a lull in the chaos.

"At the hospital. Marie's having the baby."

That news started a buzz among the customers. It was several minutes before he could get another word in. "What about the other employees?"

"They're all family. They're at the hospital, too."

He frowned. "That does not sound like good business sense to me."

"And a prince knows about these things?"

"Most certainly. I have a degree from Harvard to prove it." Abandoning the mop, he tossed a paper towel on the floor and used the sole of his shoe to finish blotting the moisture.

"Well, file that fancy degree." She glanced over his shoulder. "Another wave of flower lovers just came through the door."

"A full moon is my guess." Stooping, he picked up the damp towel.

"For what?"

"The influx of customers. There is documentation that people go a little loco during a full moon. Obviously, there has been a rash of insults hurled about and the guilty parties are apologizing with flowers."

"Could be." She grinned, not missing his reference to insults. "Either that or a certain prince has bought out all the other shops and this is the only one left with any decent blooms."

He inclined his head, amused, and reached for the ringing phone. "Could be."

AT THREE O'CLOCK, Marcello came in, passing out pink-banded cigars and declared the shop closed for the rest of the day in honor of the birth of his daughter. Joseph could picture himself beaming this way when Briana had the baby, and feeling especially proud, he slipped an extra five hundred francs in the cash drawer.

Briana saw him do it, threaded her arm through his

and absently kissed his shoulder. "That was sweet, but they'll pull their hair out tonight trying to make the receipts balance."

"The receipts will not balance anyway because I operated in round figures."

She squeezed his arm. "I'll give them a call. Too much money is easier to explain than not enough." Once outside, she looked around. "See, you gave me your car and now you're stuck on foot."

"I came in a limousine because I expected *you* to have the vehicle here."

"That's what you get for thinking."

"Silly of me."

Her laughter rang out. "Just as well. I love walking through the village."

"Perhaps it will serve as a starting point for our quest."

The reminder dimmed her pleasure in the afternoon bustle and brought back the jolt of shame, the swirl of turmoil that made her feel as if her life were balanced on a taut high-wire.

She hid the emotions, pasting a smile on her face—a smile that turned genuine when she noticed the earnestness with which Joseph searched the crowd.

"I cannot imagine a man not seeking you out," he said. It gave him a punch in the gut to think about her with another man, but her lack of memory of it diluted his jealousy somehow.

"Maybe he doesn't know how to find me. Criminy, maybe he doesn't *want* to."

"Your first statement was more valid. We will simply walk the streets, I think."

"Joseph, I object to that image on principle alone."

He frowned. "Explain."

"You make me sound like a streetwalker." When he continued to frown, she said, "A woman of ill repute?"

His brows shot up. "Ah, no, *querida*, that was not my meaning."

She laughed at his seriousness, and took a playful swipe at his arm.

One corner of his mouth turned up. "Striking a prince?"

"Give it up, Joey. You know I have no respect."

"Joey?" His laughter pealed. "My ancestors will roll over in their graves."

"Exactly." She concentrated on the smells of the outdoor produce market rather than the sound of Joseph's rich laughter. There were already too many things about this man that impressed her—and that put her on dangerous ground.

Every minute she allowed herself with him only added another wrinkle to an already overwrinkled life. But she couldn't seem to find the gumption to let go. She could only vow to live one day at a time.

"Do not think you are fooling me, Briana. Deliberately trying to shock me will not convince me of your unsuitability."

She shrugged, lifted a fragrant melon to her nose, and gave it a squeeze. Teasing was her only salvation. Because if she thought about their quest at any length, she might imagine herself in the role of a fallen woman, trolling for men, her on-the-fritz brain allowing her to act on some dark fantasy she didn't even know she'd had.

The image was too horrible to consider. She put the melon back and selected instead a little roundel of goat's cheese. Crystal had been craving cheese and olives lately. Maybe she would surprise her with a sackful.

Shoppers were out in force, picking over fresh fruits and vegetables and locally made condiments. The street market was the main attraction on the cobbled *cours Masséna*, and the press of bodies confirmed it.

Over a barrel of herb-flavored olives, Joseph crowded closer, bending to speak softly in her ear. "Do you know that man over there? The one grinning like a hyena?"

She looked up, her hand pausing over a bunch of asparagus.

"Oh, no." Heart thudding, she unconsciously moved closer to Joseph, trying her best to hide behind his shoulder. "That's the carpenter who's been working next door."

"I thought he looked familiar. Is there a possibility...?"

"God, I hope not."

"You know, you did have an odd reaction the other day in the kitchen."

"Surely I wouldn't have been so indiscriminate."

She darted another glance at the workman, pictured a little boy dressed in baggy overalls with a tool belt strapped to his puffed-out belly, Dumbo ears hideously large on either side of his freckled face, cheeks rounded in a perpetually goofy smile.

She shuddered, shook the ridiculous image away, touched her stomach, and silently apologized to the innocent child resting behind her palm. No way. Surely...

She gave a tentative wave back, which seemed to placate the workman because he moved on.

"It is not him," Joseph said resolutely.

Briana was still suffering from that impromptu flash her mind had just provided. "How do you know?"

"He would have approached you."

"Maybe." She reached out, lured by the fragrance of plump, ripe figs.

He tugged her forward. "Forget the figs. You are not looking."

"Yes, I am." Abandoning the stands of produce for the moment, she decided to give Joseph's experiment a fair try. Yet each man she looked at caused her mind to go off on a tangent.

Perspiration slicked her palms and her steps hastened.

She looked straight into the eyes of a tourist who looked like he'd just stepped off the rodeo circuit. He stared back, and tipped his hat. Imagination out of control now, she pictured a toddler wearing cowboy boots and chaps with pearl-handled Colts strapped at his waist.

*Get a grip, Bri!* She stopped, closed her eyes and took a deep breath, grasping for balance, feeling guilty, foolish, confused and half insane. For all she knew, she could have slept with an acquaintance or a total stranger—a tourist, perhaps.

She started to give the cowboy a second look, then noticed the scowl on Joseph's face. The sexy cowboy gave an apologetic shrug and blended in with the crowd.

That was when the foolishness of what they were doing struck her.

She smothered a giggle, heard frustration in Joseph's tone as he asked, "Anything?"

"Hardly. Every time a man looks at me like he might know me, you get all macho and prince-like and scare him off."

"I do not."

"Yes, you do."

"Perhaps you should not stare so hard."

"Isn't that the point?"

"Yes, but we want to be able to tell the difference between a man who thinks you are coming on to him and one who—"

"Who I've *already* come on to?" Oh, that sounded ugly—way too ugly to consider. Which brought her stomach right up into her mouth. She ought to be in confession rather than searching the streets.

His breath hissed out. "There's got to be an easier way to do this."

"What do you suggest? Should I walk up to every man and say, 'Excuse me, have we had sex?'"

He looked as horrified as she felt. Hooking her arm through his, she propelled him along the street and away from the market. Away from this ridiculous experiment.

"This was your idea," she reminded.

"Only because you insist on having answers."

"You should want those answers, too, Joseph." The minute she said the words, she regretted them. If her mind was blocking the incident because it was too horrible to deal with, wouldn't it affect Joseph the same way? He offered her unconditional acceptance, but would he still if the answers to her quest proved unacceptable?

The pain that sliced through her made her voice tremble. "On second thought, maybe we should just give it up."

"No." He stopped abruptly, pulled her to him, and rested against a stout rampart that protected the village from the sea.

Pulse skittering, she stood between his spread legs, stiff at first, then gave up the fight and settled into him. He seemed to know that she needed a moment, sensed her turmoil, and just held her, letting her absorb his strength.

She'd already told herself she would enjoy him for the remaining time he was here. It was a selfish decision, and she tried to feel guilty for feeling desire, for wanting to press closer, but the desire was too strong. Neither guilt nor reason could kill it. She needed this utter acceptance—*needed it* more than she wanted to admit.

"Better?" he asked softly.

She shook her head, then nodded, feeling confused and tortured and desperate all at once. Tightening her arms around his waist, she held him closer, wishing away the baby, the world, faceless men who might or might not have made her pregnant—wished away every single thing except Joseph.

His lips pressed against her temple, sending her heartbeat tripping. She pulled back and gazed into his eyes.

"You really should give up on me, Joseph."

"Never."

From the corner of her eye, she caught a swift movement. They turned at the same time. A man ran toward them, camera clicking.

*Oh, no.* The paparazzi had finally caught up with him. Unnerved, she jerked away, trying to duck behind him.

Joseph didn't appear surprised, just annoyed.

"What's the lady's name?" the photographer shouted, skirting cars, ignoring the blare of horns from irate drivers. "Is this serious? Is it over with the Santiago heiress?" The questions were fired on the run.

"Joseph...don't answer," she whispered, her insides quaking. "Let's just get out of here."

He hooked an arm around her waist and drew her back to his side. "They'll only hound us."

She hid her face, her voice desperate and shaking. "Just let me go. You can still save your reputation."

"My reputation does not need saving. I have nothing to hide, Briana."

"But *I* do! My family will see the pictures. They don't know about the baby. About you. *Your* family will see this." She tugged at his restraining arm, feeling irrational, as if a snapshot splashed across a tabloid would spill her secret. Knowing, regardless, that it would ruin Joseph—or at the very least cause him distress; it would make it necessary for him to run damage control, lest his country lose faith in him.

"Shh. I am used to this sort of thing. And the baby is only between you and me, for now. There will be no press leaks until well after we have told your family. And mine." He squeezed her hand. "It will be fine."

"No, it won't." Aside from the baby, her sense of fair play rose. "If you won't think about yourself, at least think about Raquel."

"I try not to."

"That's ugly."

"No. It is not important."

"Right, it's so unimportant that your brother comes looking for you."

There was no time for a response. The cameraman had successfully dodged the boulevard traffic. He prudently stopped several yards away, breath huffing, obviously concerned with celebrities taking potshots at both him and his equipment. "Care to make a comment for the *France-Soir?*"

Briana recognized the name of a popular newspaper. She shook her head, turned her back and moved a pace away, although Joseph still held her hand, preventing escape.

His voice was tight, low and threatening, nothing at all like his whispered assurances. Here was a man used to being in control, to issuing commands and having them obeyed. "I would prefer to buy that film."

"No can do, Prince Joseph. I've been covering the seven-hundredth anniversary of the Grimaldi rule in Monte Carlo. It's on this roll." He patted the camera, tightening his hand around both the strap and the Nikon.

"Then I am not such worthy news."

"Are you kidding? Prince Andrew of Monaco and

Prince Joseph of Valldoria in the same day? I could get a bonus.''

''I will pay triple that bonus for you to hold those pictures.''

Although greed gave the cameraman pause, career aspirations appeared stronger. Joseph had been afraid of that. The *France-Soir* wasn't as hungry for unsubstantiated gossip as a slipshod tabloid might be.

''I am a reasonable man,'' Joseph bargained. ''And I understand your desire to further your career.'' With his free hand, he reached for his wallet. ''In exchange for your cooperation in destroying these pictures you have taken today, I will vow to give you an exclusive in two weeks' time, complete with authorized photographs.''

''So it *is* serious.''

''Yes.''

Briana groaned.

''I don't want your money,'' the photographer said. ''I just want a story.''

''And you will have it—if you will give us privacy now.'' He urged Briana forward, away from the ready camera lens.

''Take my card, then,'' the man shouted after them.

''I know you. I will contact you.''

The photographer didn't pursue them, but Briana's nerves still screamed. ''Will he print them?''

''I have dealt with André before. He has scruples.''

That wasn't the assurance she sought. ''How do you get used to people looking at you all the time?'' She concentrated on putting one foot in front of the other, taking comfort from Joseph's protective arm around her shoulders, feeling guilty about that comfort. It put him in a bad position. No telling how many other photographers were lurking in the bushes.

"Most of the time I pay no attention. Other times, it hits me and I realize it is part of my life—a part that I did not choose." His voice grew weary. "Circumstances of my birth did not give me a choice. I was born with a title, which has never allowed me to say, 'Stop, this isn't what I want.'"

She glanced at him. "So it does bother you?"

"Recently. It is one of the reasons I came to Monte Carlo in the first place."

"I thought you said that was because of the called-off betrothal—the one your family isn't certain you've actually called off."

"The discontent has been building for quite some time."

"You were bored?" In that case, was she really just a distraction for him? Men said pretty words they didn't mean all the time.

"I have a very full life, Briana. Perhaps I was bored. Lonely, I think, is a better definition."

Her heart softened. "How can you be lonely when you're surrounded by so many people?"

"Easily, when those people are merely revolving around me. They touch me on the surface, but not deep within." His fingers moved from her shoulder to the back of her neck, beneath the fall of her hair. "A hundred people could not make me feel what you did with that very first brush of your lips."

"You're just not used to women dropping their purses at your feet." She didn't think it wise to get into accidental kisses at the moment.

His brows rose. "It has been tried on occasion."

She kept forgetting this man was a sought-after prince, an excellent catch by anyone's standards. "What made me so different?"

"That, I cannot explain. *Coup de foudre* is the best I can do."

"Love at first sight is a myth."

His palm tightened at the back of her neck in a gentle squeeze of forgiveness for the interruption he chose to ignore. "The moment our lips brushed I knew I was kissing destiny. The storm raging inside me quieted and all the missing pieces fell into place."

He made it sound so easy. So right. Franco's villa was just up ahead, her own apartment in sight. "I wish my own missing pieces would fall into place."

"As do I, Briana." He stopped her, turned her to face him. "Because until then, I do not have your full attention."

She knew his intent even before his head lowered, before his lips touched hers. She saw it in the darkening of his eyes and tried to stop him.

"Joseph, no." The words were pushed to the back of her throat as he nibbled at her lower lip. She tried again. "We've already been caught at this once."

"I do not care if the whole world sees," he said in a gritty whisper. Nonetheless, he pulled her behind a hedge, and looked straight into her eyes. "I want your full attention, Briana Duvaulle. And I mean to have it."

# Chapter Eleven

Oh, he had her attention, all right. The hunger that thickened his voice was palpable, as was her own. His need excited her as much as everything else about him did.

It was a salve on the guilt and conflict that followed her like a shadow.

The knot in her stomach grew tighter, making her shake with the tension of it. He took her face in his hands and whispered soft kisses top to bottom, surprising her with the gentleness that in no way matched the tone of his resolute promise, nor the taut muscles bunched under his knit shirt.

He smelled like the most exquisite fantasy—clean and male and sexy—and tasted even better. In the fading light of afternoon, he turned her mindless, into a creature of sensation with little room for thought or reason.

She felt heat and need as he took the kiss deeper, softer still, wetter. Her hands clutched against his chest, knotting his shirt, her knees weak. She felt the wild beating of his heart beneath her palm. Yet he held her gently.

Fragmented rational thought finally pierced the haze of desire, reminding her that anyone could walk by and see them. They were taking too many chances; too much was at stake.

She eased back, allowed her lips to cling for just another moment. "We have to stop," she whispered brokenly.

Joseph felt a kind of panic he wasn't used to. With his hands still bracketing her face, he looked into her warm green eyes, saw the reserve he couldn't fight, couldn't order or buy away.

"I cannot let you go, *querida.*" She engaged his mind. She complemented him, brought joy to his days. And damn it, he brought it to hers. He knew he did. Yet she held back.

"If you don't let me go now, Joseph, it'll just be all the harder when the time comes."

"We have time. You agreed to let me help you."

She shook her head. "I don't think that's possible. Today was a total wash."

"You are not a quitter, Briana."

"No? How do you know? How do *I* know? Lately, I don't know who or what I am."

He pulled her right back into his arms, pressed her cheek to his neck, and just held her, letting her feed off his strength, his love, helpless to do anything more. He tried to understand her desperation, but couldn't. He'd never lost an entire day of his life—a day that had resulted in life-altering consequences.

And his own needs were making the turmoil she faced even harder. She was so compassionate, so concerned over the impact she might have on his life.

He thought of telling her the impact he would suffer if she left him would be devastating, but didn't want to add to her burdens. So he just held her, rocked her gently, his gaze focused on the hedge of oleander, his senses filled with the raspberry essence of her silky hair.

"We'll still see each other," he said. "Give me that much."

"Joseph…"

"We'll find your answers, Briana. You said you'd let me help. I will not pressure you in any physical way."

She pulled back and looked at him. "What if I pressure you?"

His lips twitched. "I will make you behave."

Amusement sparked in her green eyes, banishing some of the shadows. "My parents would tell you that's a hopeless task."

"I am up to the challenge." It would probably be the death of him, but he would give it a damned good shot. In the meantime, he would give her a little space and put a plan of action together.

THE PHONE WOKE HER at an indecent hour. Her stomach roiled, but settled soon enough. When the doorbell rang, she shoved her arms into a terry-cloth robe and marched through the front room. She knew exactly who it was.

"Good morning," Joseph said.

She almost lost her head of steam. He looked wonderful in slacks and a band-collared tan shirt. In his hand was a sack from a local bakery, the smell alone distracting her.

"I don't suppose you'd know anything about Marie's Flower Shop being closed for a couple of weeks?"

He didn't say anything, but his features took on that stubborn prince-like look that should have reminded her of their differences, yet instead made her want to hug him.

"Maybe you forgot," she said sweetly. "It seems a certain person with more money than sense gave a baby gift—enough money so the proud parents could close their store for a month and devote their time to the new bundle of joy? Ring any bells?"

"They deserve time with their child. May I come in?"

"Joseph, that's my job you just shut down." She stepped back, told herself not to respond to the sight of his bronze hand against the white bakery bag, and made a herculean effort to drag her gaze back up to his.

"Did they not tell you that you would be paid regardless?"

"Yes." She sighed, and collapsed on the sofa. "Nobody gives paid vacations to a one-day employee."

"They do now."

"Why?" She reached for the bakery bag.

"Because we have things to do and we need time in order to do them."

"Joseph, I can't take your money."

"You aren't."

"Yes, I am...or would be. You've paid them to close the store. In turn, that money will go to pay my wages. Wages that I'm not earning."

"And it is so important to you to earn your way?"

"Very."

"What about the memory thing?"

"That's important, too. But I'm used to standing alone."

"You do not have to."

"You don't understand." Her hand fisted around the bag. "It's so easy for you."

"If I have the money to spare, what is the problem?"

"My sense of self. I don't want to live in anyone's shadow."

"I'm not asking you to. And our situation is different."

Because love was involved. She looked away, and drew a croissant out of the bag. "I told Marcello my salary would be an additional contribution to their baby."

"You are the most stubborn woman."

She smiled. "It's a curse."

"Fine, then. I will call him and pay him to reopen the store."

"Joseph, you don't have to pay him. I've already told him I'll be back in on Monday—regardless."

He watched her for a long moment. "That gives us the weekend, then."

"To find my lost mind."

"Your mind is not lost."

"One day of it is."

"And we will get it back."

"By the look on your face, I gather you have a suggestion?"

"Yes. We must re-create the day."

She gave a short laugh, nearly choked on the buttery roll. "You might want to think twice. It was a bizarre day, even by my standards."

"So you remember parts of it?"

"Parts. The starting point. Events that led up to it. That's all."

"And they were?"

"A fertility rock."

BRIANA'S NERVES WERE all over the place. She kept expecting men to jump out of the bushes, claiming carnal knowledge of her person.

It gave her the willies, made her sick to her stomach. She wasn't sure if it was the altitude or repressed memories that shortened her breath. A brisk breeze whipped at her hair, flattening her skirt against her thighs.

"Relax," Joseph said, leading her along a pathway that meandered through an alpine meadow ablaze with bellflowers and edelweiss, his palm reassuring and warm at her back.

"Easy for you to say."

"Does anything look familiar?"

"Yes. This much of it, I remember." Beyond the arched, fourteenth-century gateway, the landscape thickened into a majestic forest that enveloped them in the smell of pine and wild lavender. And just beyond, through the darkened canopy of foliage, was a wide ray of light that seemed to shine down from the heavens.

As she had before, Briana felt as if that slice of illumination were calling to her, drawing her forward like the ancient chanting of a mythical world. Logically she knew the fine specks swirling in that beam were atmospheric particles. Fancifully, she imagined them to be fairy dust.

After all, this was a place touted to be magical—a place where people came to indulge in healing rituals and to pray for babies. Not her thing, but hey, who was she to judge?

"Where are the springs you mentioned?"

"You'll see. That beam of light is coming from a tunnel-like area. Past that are the waterfalls and springs and rocks."

"Fertility rock. What exactly is that?"

She shot him an amused look, and repeated, "You'll see."

And he did. Mouth open, staring. Smooth-faced cliffs formed an open-air circle around them. Where the forest had been chilly, this grotto-like area was sultry and damp, coating their skin and clothes with a fine mist in a matter of minutes. In search of prey, a magnificent falcon circled overhead, casting shadows over the stone surfaces.

Rather than in an angry crash, a waterfall spilled gently over jutting rocks, trickling into a lagoon. Exotic ferns and blossoms sprouted at will in and around the outcropping.

All in all, a peaceful, restful setting.

Joseph's astonishment came from the huge, phallic-shaped rock jutting straight up from the center of the viridescent pool.

"That," Briana said, "is what we call a fertility rock."

Joseph cleared his throat, continued to stare. "No children under thirteen unless accompanied by a parent," he said inanely.

"More like under twenty-one. The keepers of this place don't advocate children having children."

"Where are they, by the way?"

"The keepers?"

"And other people. The place appears deserted."

"There's a building just outside the opening we passed through that has telephones and bathrooms. It's pretty well hidden by the forest and you'd miss it if you weren't looking for it. In any case, this isn't a tourist attraction. Very few people know about it." She shrugged. "Some days, it's crawling with people, and some days it's not."

"Yet you said you were offered a drink when you were here. Has someone capitalized on this spot of nature?" And what a spot it was. Perhaps it was his imagination run wild from the sight of that jutting rock, but on closer inspection, he noted the formation of the cliffs—realized that what appeared to be dips and hollows now took on the shape of the feminine form.

"There's no charge to be here, if that's what you mean. Each generation of villagers sort of looks after the place. Evidently somebody came up with the idea that an aphrodisiac potion increased the fertility process, so the recipe has been handed down through generations and someone is always available to provide it." She glanced at him, held up a hand. "Don't ask me what's in it. That's the last thing I remember."

"What did it taste like?"

She shrugged. "Pineapple juice."

"And where did you drink it?"

"Sitting in the pool."

"Were there others sitting with you?"

"Quite a few that day. I'm a little surprised there isn't anyone here today."

"Were there other men?"

"I think so. Husbands or sweethearts, maybe."

"Single ones that you recall?"

"I told you I recall very little. I only came because it was so important to Crystal. Actually, I thought it was kind of stupid, but Crystal's been really desperate on the subject of babies lately."

"Why?" He dragged his gaze away from the sight of slick stone breasts midway up the canyon wall, with water trickling in and around the erotic formations. This place had a way of filling the mind and senses with carnal thoughts. He wasn't sure about the praying-for-babies part, but he was damned sure about couples leaving here and heading straight for the nearest bed; or at the very least, a spot for privacy.

"Because she's not using any form of birth control and she's never gotten pregnant. Franco wants to marry her, but she won't agree until she's assured she can give him children."

"Is that one of his requirements?" He wasn't sure he would care for such a man.

"No. He wants Crystal any way he can get her. It's her hang-up."

Franco went back up in Joseph's esteem. And he could certainly identify with wanting a woman any way he could get her. He wanted Briana with an ache that went soul deep. An ache that was now straining against his pants.

"So your cousin wanted to come here to the, uh…the rock, to pray for a baby." He stared at the giant penis formation standing proudly in the center of the pool, and figured there weren't too many men who would willingly come here. The size of the thing would intimidate even the most self-assured male, although his own erection felt like it was damned close to measuring up.

"That's about the size of it."

His head whipped around and his lips twitched at the impish expression on her face.

She laughed, the sound echoing off the walls of the grotto. "Call it what it is, Joseph. A giant rock penis. Or does that offend your proper, princely sensibilities?"

He stepped closer, pinning her with a look that made her breath snag. "On the contrary. I am considering having my mason visit for inspiration."

She bit her lip. "Your mother might find it a bit tacky to add a penis-shaped fountain that spouts water."

"Who said anything about a fountain? There is a custom among the Castillos that dates back several generations. When the heir to the throne reaches the age of thirty, masons carve his likeness in a statue."

She went off into another peal of laughter. "Your ego is astonishing."

"Healthy," he corrected, drawing her to him, cutting off her laughter in a manner that took the starch out of her backbone and turned her knees to jelly.

His lips were warm and moist from the sultry mist that surrounded them. By the time he drew back, she had trouble catching her breath.

"You are so beautiful."

Her clothes were damp and clinging, her hair probably frizzed from the humidity, yet she didn't doubt his words. It always amazed her that he found her beautiful. She was taller than average, in no way fashionably thin, and although her features could be considered above average, she wasn't a striking beauty.

But his eyes, his touch, his voice, told her that he thought so. It was sweet, uplifting; a fantasy of the highest order.

She cleared her throat and stepped back. "We're getting sidetracked. And we're not really making any headway."

"I thought we were doing quite well."

"I meant with the memory thing."

He watched her with indulgence in his eyes. "I know what you mean."

Nerves crowded in, making her words tumble out recklessly. "You'd think a phallus-shaped rock would spark *something*."

"You'd think."

Her eyes skimmed down the front of his pants, widened at the sight of the arousal he couldn't hide, then snapped back up. That *wasn't* the spark she'd meant.

His gaze never left her face. A dimple creased his cheek, his sensual lips curved in the barest hint of a smile. He seemed the most delighted when she was the least proper—which was most of the time.

Somebody needed to give this man a refresher course in princely standards and expectations. She didn't meet either and he was blind if he couldn't see that.

Heart pumping so hard it made her dizzy, she threw up her hands and whirled around. If she kept looking at him, she would beg him to strip and jump in that pool with her. Which might not be a bad idea. If the place was magic, it might be able to change the paternity of this baby.

And she was seriously losing it, she decided.

"It's no use, Joseph. I might be thinking about sex, but none that I had on that day."

"I like it that you are thinking about sex. With me, no doubt."

"No doubt," she mumbled.

"What does Crystal say?"

"To go for it."

"I like her more and more. I meant about what the two of you did when you were here last."

Her face flamed. "Oh." *Get a grip, Briana. Please.* "She said I drank the pineapple juice, got woozy and called a cab and went home."

"And she *let* you go alone when you were feeling ill?"

"She tried to stop me, but I was adamant, I guess. Evidently I told her I didn't want to spoil the possibilities for her. There was a woman speaking that day, a healer. Crystal had her heart set on talking to her.''

Joseph raised a brow. ''A healer? I must admit, I'm skeptical about that concept.''

''That surprises me since you're so accepting of *my* weird circumstances.'' He'd never questioned her sanity or her claims.

''You have not given me a weird explanation.''

''No. Just *no* explanation.''

He stared at their surroundings as if the answers were etched in the stone. ''Obviously, something in the potion you drank did not mix well with your body chemistry—''

''The antihistamine I took is my guess.''

He nodded. ''Thus the memory loss.''

''Yeah, and sometime during that memory loss I got myself pregnant.'' She looked at the pool, wondered if it was stocked with little sperm swimming below the surface, sort of the way people stocked lakes with trout. The thought was ludicrous and didn't bear voicing.

Then again, this whole situation was ludicrous.

She wondered if Joseph might even be entertaining the same thoughts. He was staring at the phallic rock with a great deal of speculation, until the cellular phone in his pocket rang, causing her to jump.

''A phone call?'' she said, grinning. ''In the middle of nowhere?''

Joseph wondered about the same thing. Obviously they weren't too far from civilization, though, because a ringing phone meant they were within range of a cell site.

He sent Briana an apologetic look and turned his back, the move putting his line of vision right smack on the fertility rock in a way that made it look as if it were barely kissing the entrance of a soft vee in the cliff face—the womanly vee of a female form.

"Joseph?"

*"Madre."* There was no way his mother could know what he was staring at right this moment, but embarrassment jolted through him nonetheless. Sweat clung to the line of his spine, beaded at his temple; his voice was a raspy croak. "I cannot speak at the moment."

He heard Briana's giggle, knew she realized his dilemma, and jerked his gaze away from the jutting stone, shooting her a quelling look that carried little impact.

"Are you unwell, my son?"

"I am fine—"

"Because if you are, I should know about it. There is a wedding being planned. Duties to attend to. You have sent Max and Pedro home—and it was *bad* of you to threaten Maximilianus so."

"Mother..." He started to tell her to cancel the wedding plans, but decided not to get into that can of worms. Besides, if all went well, he would be bringing home a true betrothed—one of his own choosing. All the better if there was a jump on the wedding plans.

"I am quite well," he said instead, addressing each of her statements and questions. "And I am aware of my duties. Max is a big boy—he can take a few threats. I do not need a bodyguard...." He lowered his voice, pitched his tone in a manner he knew his mother had never been able to resist. "And you of all people know that I am bad."

"Teasing the queen is in poor taste, my son." He heard her reluctant amusement. "You have undoubtedly picked up more bad habits?"

"And some good ones." Briana was a habit his mother would love, but he couldn't discuss his feelings over a cellular phone. That would have to be done in person. He just hoped his mother's sense of fair play would be enough to overcome tradition. "I have to go, Mother. I am in the middle of..." His gazed darted from the rock to Briana. "Something," he finished, and stabbed the End button just as Briana burst forth with another giggle.

"You enjoyed that, didn't you?" he asked, his lips climbing in a grin that was becoming another habit. A good one.

"Let's just say I wouldn't want to be talking to *my* mother here."

"She'd send you to the nuns, huh?"

"She still might do that, once she finds out the mess I've gotten into."

"No, a *princesa* must live in the palace, not the convent."

"I'm not a princess."

"We will resume that debate once we have solved your memory puzzle."

"It doesn't look like it's solvable." Frustration grew, attacking her insides like a swarm of stinging bees. While Joseph had been busy on the phone, another couple had entered the grotto. The sight of them stroking both the feminine and masculine formations of stone was simply too much.

Desire was screaming at a fever pitch. Is this what she'd felt that day? Had the stimulation been so great that she'd hopped in a cab and snagged the first willing victim she could get her hands on?

It was a possibility she didn't want to consider, but one that wouldn't let go. Her insides throbbed, and her breasts felt swollen. She could feel her heart beat in every pulse point in her body, and like an obsession, she wanted.

*Wanted* with a desperation that threatened to erupt in a scream. Here. Now. With Joseph.

Only with Joseph.

Lord have mercy, she needed to get out of here. Another minute and memory quests would go right by the wayside. Resolute vows to stay out of his bed would vanish like dust motes at the jerk of a curtain.

"Let's get out of here."

THE DREAM STOLE INTO her subconscious, while she was gently, vividly, drifting along in that state where she might have been half-awake, yet couldn't drag her eyes open.

Marble floors stretched out like a sea of glass below her. She wore a ball gown in soft yellow, skirts billowing with the aid of yards of stiff netting, trailing against the silk runner of the sweeping staircase, glass slippers catching the light of enormous chandeliers as her dainty feet found graceful purchase on each descending step.

She paused, marveling at how the magic shoes had

transformed her size-ten feet down to a feminine six. Warmth glowed in her stomach, in her heart, growing stronger as she looked up and saw Joseph waiting at the bottom of the stairs in the great hall.

Beside him stood a tiny boy of two, with dark hair and cherub cheeks set with dimples. A miniature crown perched on his head, and a tiny robe in platinum and black swept from his shoulders, marking him as royalty.

Her son.

The happiness that swelled in her bosom at the sight of the two most important people in her life was almost too much to contain. She reached out a hand, but was too far away to touch.

Suddenly the steps appeared longer—an escalator now, pulling her back, adding three steps to each two she tried to take.

The child's face, a face that should have been full of innocence and glee, appeared tortured. Scared.

Why was her baby scared?

She tried to run, tried to call out to Joseph to pick him up. Something was wrong. Her baby needed protection. But the stairs thwarted her, pulling her away instead of closer.

Faces crowded into the hall, bearing down on her son, pushing Joseph out of the way.

"No!" she screamed, desperate to reach her child, to reach Joseph. Desperate to guard her secrets, her shame; to guard the innocence of her child.

But nobody listened. Nobody came to her baby's aid.

Joseph tried, but the mob held him back.

Briana tried, but the stairs moved faster.

She was dizzy from the force of her heartbeat, the churning of her stomach, the raw ache in her throat as she continued to scream. Helpless to reach her child, to save him from emotional harm, from the repercussions of her selfish choice.

The child never took his eyes off his mother.

Hands reached for the tiny boy, snatching at the crown, stripping him of the little robe. "Imposter," they chanted.

Naked now, the baby stood alone in the great hall, fear and shame in his dark eyes—wise eyes, she realized—with fat tears spilling over the rims, slipping silently over chubby cheeks....

BRIANA JERKED UPRIGHT in the bed, felt her stomach heave. She thrust aside the blankets and ran for the bathroom. Aside from the remnants of the nightmare, Briana, who'd prided herself as being one of those women blessed to escape morning sickness, now woke up to it with a vengeance.

And with her head hanging indignantly over the toilet, she cried. For herself, for the baby, for her absent memory, for her guilty thoughts—and most of all, for Joseph.

Because he could never be hers to hold.

He'd said he was staying a month. He'd been here for six weeks.

Already, ten days had passed since their trip to the fertility springs, and they were no closer to capturing her elusive memory blip than before.

The days were moving faster. Time was her enemy.

Soon she would begin to show. She had to think about Joseph's reputation even if he refused to do so.

She should have known better; *had* known better. She'd cautioned herself not to get in deeper. Now it was guaranteed that her heart would break when he went back to his duties.

She felt a cool cloth at her head, gentle hands holding her hair. Each night Joseph slept with her, held her. Yet they hadn't made love since the night on the yacht. He respected her confusion, but insisted it didn't mean he couldn't wake up to her in the mornings.

And when it came to Joseph Castillo, she was a marshmallow and she couldn't find the strength to send him away.

Now, however, was a different matter. She was horrified.

"Go away."

He ignored the plea, continued to stroke her hair, her cheeks, held the cloth to her forehead. She sighed, and snapped the toilet lid closed, rising shakily to her feet with the solicitous aid of Joseph's hands.

"Now I've done it all," she moaned, grabbing a bottle of mouthwash.

"What's that?"

"Thrown up in the presence of a prince." She swished the minty liquid in her mouth, avoided his reflection in the bathroom mirror. "Bet you've never had *that* happen."

"There is a first time for everything. And you have good reason." He urged her out of the bathroom, his arm steady around her.

Embarrassment couldn't keep her gaze from straying. She looked at his sleepy features, felt the warmth of his bare chest against her side, felt her stomach give a giddy leap at the sight of his unsnapped jeans. A moan escaped before she could call it back.

He halted, and started to turn back toward the bathroom. "Again?" he asked, gentle compassion etched in his dark eyes.

"No. I'll be fine if I just lie down for another minute or two." *I hope.* She didn't want to repeat that experience anytime soon.

He helped her into bed, then hovered. "Can I get you something? Tea? Crackers?"

She shook her head, and crooked an arm over her eyes. Hiding. Begging her stomach not to revolt again. "Just give me a minute. Then I'll get up and get ready for work."

"Briana, you cannot go to work in this condition."

She lowered her arm, looked at him. "Yes, I can. And if you call and pay to have the store closed again, I won't be responsible for my actions."

His brows lifted. "What will you do?"

"I haven't decided yet. But rest assured, it'll hurt."

He grinned. "My fierce little princess."

"I'm not a princess and I'm not little." And she felt more wimpy than fierce.

"You are the perfect princess."

"Right. I can drive the queen in your limo, skate through your halls with a gold serving tray balanced on my palm—"

"Platinum."

"Answer the palace phone...in several languages if need be."

"See there? With only a minor adjustment from gold to platinum—you really must respect our metal—you have listed some excellent qualities and qualifications. As I said, perfect."

She brought her arm down all the way, scooted up in the bed, pleased that her stomach no longer objected to movement. "Are you delusional, or what?"

"There you go, insulting the prince again," he teased.

"Joseph—"

"Tell me something. Were you not the best waitress on roller skates?"

"Well...yes."

"And the best limousine driver?"

"I never dented a fender," she allowed grudgingly.

"I talked to you myself on the phone when you were at the consulate. Your voice was melodious, your manners impeccable."

She rolled her eyes. "Now I know you're delusional. I hung up on you."

"True. But I caught you off guard. My point is, each position you have held in no way takes away from your suitability to be a princess of my country. Each job was a learning experience, adding to your life résumé. That makes you more qualified than someone who has spent her life behind the sheltered walls of a castle. You are engaging and can talk commonplace or heavy-duty politics with—"

"Oh, *please*, don't let me do that. I'd insult an ally and send your country to war."

"Ah, no, *querida.* Your beauty alone would dazzle even the nastiest foe. You were, after all, a Paris model."

She pounced on that. "Not the best."

"But damned good," he countered.

"Yes. Damned good." She allowed a tiny smile, felt tears of emotion back up in her throat. He was a prince in more than title. He celebrated her, let her know that her best would always be good enough in his eyes.

A woman could search a lifetime and never find half the support and encouragement and love that Joseph offered.

Never find a man so utterly, genuinely determined in his pursuit of love.

## Chapter Twelve

She came home for lunch, feeling shaky from her bout of morning sickness, from the snatches of the nightmare that kept surprising her at unguarded moments, and needing the encouragement of family around her.

Joseph was wearing her down.

Dreams didn't mean anything, did they?

The missing day of her life was still a total blank. Joseph had suggested hypnosis. But, ridiculously, that scared her more than remembering on her own.

She figured she would run the idea by Crystal and get her cousin's thoughts on the subject.

When she let herself into the villa, she found Crystal curled up in the middle of the couch. Sobbing.

Flamboyant, unflappable, sunny Crystal was crying. Terrified, Briana rushed over.

"What is it?"

Crystal cried harder.

"Crys, talk to me." She smoothed back the wild tumble of blond hair, wiped at the tears, hugged her, felt her own eyes fill as horrors raced through her mind. "Is it Franco? Your mom...*my* mom?"

Crystal shook her head, held up a plastic stick.

Briana frowned, and glanced from the stick to the box resting in Crystal's lap.

A home pregnancy test.

She grabbed Crystal's hand, held the stick closer, inspected the color, the double lines indicating positive results. Her heart gave a glad leap.

"Crystal? Oh, Crystal! You're pregnant!"

"Yes." Her clear blue eyes still spouted copious tears. Happy tears. Tears of joy and relief. "I am almost afraid to believe. After all, this is only a home test. It is not infallible."

Briana jumped to her feet. "I'm taking you to the doctor. It's time for me to have a checkup, anyway. We'll kill two birds with one stone. Wait right here." She raced through the villa, out the back door and across the breezeway to her own quarters. Once in her bedroom, she rummaged through her dresser for the slip of paper she'd been avoiding for entirely too long.

Maybe the reason she'd been so reluctant to make the initial doctor's appointment was because of Crystal. Crystal who wanted a baby so badly. Briana realized that she'd felt guilty about that; guilty that *she'd* been the one to get pregnant instead.

And because of that, she'd been reluctant to have prenatal literature and starter kits thrust on her, to take the chance that Crystal would stumble on them and suffer the emotional pain all over again.

Now it was safer to accept those things, to spend the ensuing months under a doctor's care. She and Crystal would do it together. And it would be fine.

She picked up the phone and called for an appointment. She fudged a bit, making it sound like an emergency. The receptionist said there might be a bit of a wait, but she could squeeze them in that afternoon—provided nobody went into labor unexpectedly.

Briana crossed her fingers, then dialed the flower shop and requested the rest of the day off.

THEY'D BOTH HAD an examination, and now sat in the doctor's private office, clutching hands like schoolgirls waiting to see if each had made the cheerleading squad.

Dr. Lebourn came around the desk, two files in front of him. "The Mademoiselles Duvaulles," he greeted, perching half spectacles on his nose. "Cousins, I understand?"

"Yes," they chimed in unison, causing the doctor to smile.

"Well, then. We have Crystal at fifteen weeks and Briana at a tiny glimmer of six weeks."

"No," Briana corrected. "*I'm* the further along."

"What would give you that impression?" The doctor frowned, glanced at his notes, then at each woman.

"I got a notice from your office after my last exam."

His frown deepened, making Briana's stomach swirl. Papers rustled as he flipped them back, shuffled between the two files—one marked, C. Duvaulle, the other marked B. Duvaulle. Then his gray hairline shifted.

He pulled a carbon copy of the notice Briana had received.

Pulled it from Crystal's file.

"I remember the two of you in here before."

"On the same day," Briana agreed.

"But I only examined you," he said to Briana, then shifted his gaze to Crystal. "Crystal, your cousin was in for a urinary infection, yet you gave a specimen, too?"

Crystal nodded. "Since I don't have normal periods...I had hoped." She shrugged. "I asked the nurse to run a pregnancy test."

"Which the lab did." He removed his glasses and leaned back in his chair. "And since Briana was the patient that day, the results and report were typed up and sent in her name."

Briana swayed, clutched harder at Crystal's hand, her heart pounding. "What are you saying?" she whispered. "That I wasn't pregnant then?"

"Not then. You had a simple bacterial infection. Now, however, is another matter. The pelvic examination I just performed indicates, unquestionably, that you are six weeks along."

*Six weeks.* Six weeks ago, she'd met Joseph.

And made love with him.

She heard a buzzing in her ears, felt herself go boiling hot, then icy cold. Heard the scrape of a chair, the rushing of footsteps, Crystal's frantic voice, the abrasive, jolting smell of ammonia.

She inhaled, and coughed, pushing at the hands that held the vile smelling-salts under her nose. "I'm fine. I'm fine."

"Good heavens, Briana. You were slipping right out of that chair and taking me with you."

"Sorry," Briana said to her cousin. "I guess I'm a little shocked."

And relieved. She hadn't done anything stupid, after all. At least, not on the day they'd gone to the springs. Evidently she'd gone home and slept alone, like a good girl.

There wasn't a wannabe floozy lurking in her subconscious as she'd feared.

Her hand pressed against her stomach, where butterflies still swarmed in fluttering chaos.

A baby.

Joseph's baby.

Here were the emotions she should have felt all along. The grinning-from-ear-to-ear, leap-for-joy, shout-from-the-rooftops kind of joy.

Then sanity took over the euphoria. How could she tell him? He would think she was a nut, think she'd been playing games with him. To go from claiming memory loss and pregnancy—when there was none—to pregnancy for real—a result of their very first night together.

When she thought about it, though, she was inclined to give Joseph more credit. He was a unique man. A trusting man.

Too trusting, at times.

Still, she needed to think about it, figure out just the right way to present the news to him. She'd lost her way for a while, but Joseph had found her, held her when she'd threatened to fall, believed, had celebrated…loved.

Taken her right to the edge of heaven. With this new development, she might just make it all the way through the gates.

THE FLOWER SHOP WAS slow. It figured, since there was extra help today. Joseph had taken a two-day trip, but was due back that evening.

Her heart gave a funny leap and the gladiolus in her hand trembled along with her giddy nerves. She'd planned his homecoming right down to the last candlestick, poring over cookbooks in search of just the right recipes. With great attention to detail, she cut daffodils, carpet roses, mums and fern stems and wrapped them in cellophane to take home. Now all that was left was a quick stop at the market for fresh asparagus.

She glanced up when the bells above the door jingled. The woman who walked in was absolutely stunning. Petite, with smooth olive skin and midnight hair shifting like a waterfall past her hips.

The man whose arm she clung to looked enough like Joseph to give Briana's heart a scare. His grin branded him as an irresistible flirt, but there was a strained quality to it. Almost apologetic.

"May I help you?" She spoke in French, deliberately, even though it was evident that the man was of Latin ancestry. A sense of foreboding swept over her.

He answered in English, his dark eyes gentling in what seemed to be understanding. "You are Briana Duvaulle."

"Yes." She glanced at the woman by his side.

"She does not speak the English language. I am Antonio Castillo."

"I thought so." She still couldn't get past the stunning beauty of the woman. "My guess would be that's Joseph's heiress?" His betrothed.

"Joseph has told you of her?"

"Some." She'd been able to convince herself she wasn't poaching on another woman's territory. Mainly because Joseph had said there were no feelings between him and the beautiful Raquel. Then again, there was the adage, Out of Sight, Out of Mind. Because she hadn't actually met the woman, Briana had chosen the ostrich route, fooling herself into believing the other woman didn't exist.

Face-to-face, she could no longer hide.

Technically, she still hadn't been introduced. Nonetheless, she felt just awful.

"I'm fluent in languages. Should we converse so Raquel can understand?"

At the mention of her name, the other woman perked up, first looking at Antonio, then to Briana. Antonio shook his head, then continued to speak in English, which seemed rude to Briana. Evidently it did to Raquel, also, because her almond-shaped eyes narrowed ever so slightly.

"Raquel's father, and my own, have decided that it would be wise for Joseph's betrothed to seek him out, perhaps see if there is a way to iron out the differences."

Briana winced, touched a hand to her stomach, the action hidden by the wooden counter between them. "He's not here."

"I thought perhaps you would know his where-abouts. The yacht is no longer in the Monte Carlo marina."

"No, he moved it to the port of Antibes."

"Ah, then we must try there."

Briana shook her head. "You won't find him. He took a flight out yesterday morning."

"Where?"

"He didn't say."

Antonio frowned. "That is unlike Joseph. He is a stickler for rules." His expression softened. "Yet there have been some changes in him lately. Due to you, I am thinking."

The foreboding turned into outright panic. She didn't respond to his softness, didn't agree or disagree about Joseph's changes. This was no polite visit for directions.

It was a subtle reminder of reality. Royal-style.

Her voice trembling with both sorrow and guilt, she could do little more than whisper. "He said the wedding wasn't going to take place. He said she didn't have feelings for him." She deliberately didn't use Raquel's name, felt low enough as it was.

Antonio shrugged. "Feelings have little to do with duty. The Santiagos are powerful people in our country. The marriage is more like a merger of two dynasties. Raquel will uphold her duty."

*And so must Joseph.*

"I've tried to let him go," she whispered.

"Unrequited love," Antonio murmured. "It's a bitch."

Did he mean her or Raquel? Her nerves were too

shaken to ask him for clarification. Her gaze darted to the beautiful heiress.

"Is she curious about me?" If the roles were reversed, Briana would be itching to scratch somebody's eyes out.

"She does not know you are the one. There was a mention in the newspaper, yet no photographs. The king, my father, however, has his own set of photos."

"How?"

"Joseph is adamant about not being shadowed by bodyguards. Others have been sent to keep tabs, to report back to my father."

Her eyes widened.

"Nothing compromising," Antonio assured. "I'm the one who's always getting caught in scandalous positions."

"But your father...the king. He's not pleased."

Antonio started to reach out, then drew his hand back. "I've never had to worry over what displeases my father. Joseph, in his position, has."

It wasn't an answer so much as an indirect couching in order to let her down softly. An apology.

All along, Briana had known of Joseph's duty. Still, she'd hoped.

And just when she'd thought there might *be* hope, a chance to grasp the dream, the rug was jerked from beneath her. The stakes were too high. Not just for her. But for Joseph.

She glanced at Raquel, the ache in her throat almost too much to bear. "Does she love him?" Her voice broke on the last note and she swallowed, fighting for balance.

The heiress, who appeared to be perfectly happy standing like a pretty statue letting them talk around her, suddenly leaned forward. Her dark eyes went from bored to shrewd in a matter of seconds, softening in compassion. So, there was substance to the woman, after all.

"It is Briana, no?" The woman spoke in Spanish and Briana answered likewise.

"Yes."

"You are acquainted with the prince?"

Briana nodded. She didn't know how to apologize—didn't know if she should. Beneath the counter, her fingers laced over her abdomen as if to shield her child's ears from whatever might be said.

Raquel held out her hand. After a moment's hesitation, Briana accepted the offering, noting the contrast with her own skin color and size. About the only common ground she and Raquel shared was gender and Joseph.

"It is difficult for me to show emotion," Raquel said softly. "All my life I have been told how to be, what to say...." She squeezed Briana's hand. "I see emotions in your eyes that I long to unleash myself. I envy you the freedom—a luxury I have never had." She glanced at Antonio. "Please, give us one moment of privacy."

He nodded, stepped several paces away.

Raquel turned back to Briana. "It is difficult to speak freely. Antonio and Prince Joseph are family." She shook her head, lifted the heavy fall of hair off her neck and let it drop. "Alas, I find that I still cannot. The extent of my defiance is wearing my hair down in public, but Antonio indulges my rare flights of rebellion.''

The undercurrents of what this woman was *not* saying fairly shouted. ''What is it, Raquel? What are you trying to tell me?''

''My father is very strong-willed and powerful. I cannot defy him. I, too, would choose another....'' She glanced over her shoulder as if expecting an army to appear and slap her in shackles for the veiled admission. ''I have said too much.''

''There's someone else in your life?''

Raquel's eyes widened. ''I did not say such a thing.''

Briana understood. Still, her curiosity got the better of her. ''Is it Antonio?''

Shock registered for a heartbeat in those eyes that could hide so much. Then Raquel laughed, proving that she wasn't an emotionless puppet, despite her rearing. ''Antonio will never be a one-woman man. He and I are like siblings, and I can trust him to understand if I act out on occasion.''

''If you weren't promised to Joseph, would you be free to see the other guy?''

Raquel's hair swung like thick strands of silk as she shook her head, her gaze once again darting furtively to the door.

''I am not free, and I cannot speak of this subject.'' She gave Briana's hand a final squeeze, then drew back. ''My heart will cry for the pain I see in your eyes. If the king decrees this marriage, despite the prince's objections, I must comply. I know my duty. I have been immersed in it since the cradle.''

Briana felt her eyes fill, and fought it back. The heiress had as much as admitted that she didn't want Joseph, but it was out of her hands.

Out of *all* their hands.

"I wish you happiness, Briana." Their eyes held for a long moment, woman to woman, each understanding their duty, the hand they'd been dealt by fate of birth. "If I had a speck of backbone, I would follow my own heart and—" She stopped abruptly, turned and spoke to Antonio—in flawless English. "We must return home now, Tony. We have obeyed Father's directive, but Prince Joseph is not here."

Briana, along with Antonio, stared. Raquel merely shrugged. "Perhaps I have more backbone than even I suspected. Ready, Antonio?"

Antonio nodded, took Raquel's elbow and gave a last apologetic glance at Briana. From his pocket, he withdrew an envelope and placed it on the counter. "I'm lucky I'm just the spare. I hate all this political crap."

Briana stared at the envelope for a long time after Antonio and Raquel had left the shop. It bore the Santiago logo entwined with the Castillos of Valldoria crest.

As if the merger of the two families was already a done deal.

Fingers trembling, she slipped open the seal and her stomach executed a sick tumble. Inside was a bank draft for more money than she could have dreamed of in a lifetime.

Payoff money.

Carefully, meticulously, she tore it in half, then half

again, placed the pieces back in the envelope, scrawled out the address of the palace and tossed it in the outgoing mail slot.

The memory of her nightmare flashed in her mind. The child resting in her womb wasn't an imposter, but neither was he or she legitimate.

Now, more than ever, she knew she could never tell Joseph about this child.

It felt as though the walls were pressing in on her. In a daze, she went to the back room, ignored the cellophane-wrapped flowers on the worktable and picked up her purse.

Marie was in the office, nursing her daughter. She looked up when Briana knocked on the open doorway.

"Come in."

Oh, the sight of that sweet child nearly brought her to her knees. She shook her head. "I need to take off for a couple of days."

Marie studied her for a moment, nodding. "Take as long as you need. You will always have a job here. Anytime."

"Thanks, Marie."

She walked home, for once not even noticing the fragrant smells of the marketplace. The Mercedes was still in the driveway. She'd refused to drive it, and Joseph had refused to take it back. Walking past it, she went into her apartment, tossed clothes into an overnight bag and grabbed a set of keys from the kitchen drawer.

Then she picked up the phone, feeling like a coward but past caring. Crystal answered on the second ring.

"Crys? Is anybody using Franco's chalet?"

"No. It is unoccupied."

"Would he mind if I went up there for a few days?"

"Bri? What is wrong?"

She was afraid she would cry, afraid Crystal would rush over and make her talk. But her emotions were too raw right now for a heart-to-heart.

She didn't have a choice. And neither did Joseph. He might be a prince, but the king still ruled. As Raquel had said, it had been decreed that the prince would wed the heiress. And, baby or not, even if Briana wanted to stand in the way of that union, it wasn't possible.

"Can I use it?" she asked again, unable to answer.

"Is it Joseph?"

Briana shook her head, realized her cousin couldn't see the gesture. "No. I haven't seen him. Can I use the place or not, Crystal?"

"Of course you can, but—"

"Please, don't worry about me. All I need is a little time. I'm feeling fragile, I've got a lot on my mind. I figure the snow-covered mountains will clear my head."

"Do you want me to go with you?"

"No. Thanks, Crys, but I really need to be alone. I'll call you."

She hung up the phone, tossed her bag into the Mercedes and reversed out of the driveway before

Crystal even realized she'd been calling from the guest apartment just yards away.

JOSEPH FELT AS THOUGH he'd been flying nonstop for the past forty-eight hours. Thank God for the Concorde. Otherwise, his mission would have taken him much longer.

The specialist in California was a friend—the best in his field. Although Briana had said her father's condition was inoperable, Joseph had had a hunch it might not be.

And his hunch had paid off. Dr. Martin Bertelli specialized in spinal-cord injuries and confirmed that Thomas Duvaulle was a perfect candidate for a new procedure he'd perfected. A very expensive procedure.

Not wanting to get Briana's hopes up, Joseph had made the trip to Ohio, talked to the Duvaulles, and paid a visit to California.

They would have the results of the tests in a week's time.

If all went well, this would be his wedding gift to Briana. To have her father *walk* her down the aisle.

Feeling tired, but good, he was just about to step into the shower when the cellular phone rang. He almost ignored it. He didn't want any more pressure from his mother—or worse, from the king.

But it could be Briana calling. So he retraced his steps, picked up his coat, and took out the portable.

"Prince? Crystal here."

He grinned. The cousin was as impudent as Briana.

Her next words, however, wiped the grin off his face and had his heart racing like a Thoroughbred's.

"Briana's headed for the hills," Crystal said shortly. "Thought you'd like to know."

"The hills?" Confusion made his tone abrupt.

"A chalet Franco owns in the mountains. It is part of one of those time share resorts," she clarified. "This is the last chance I'll give you, Prince. Hurt her, and you'll answer to me."

The woman obviously thought he'd run Briana out of town somehow. He sighed. "I don't want to hurt her. I want to marry her."

There was a pause on the other end of the phone. "Got a pen handy?"

"Yes. Fire away." He wrote down the information, pressed the disconnect button, then lifted his finger and dialed the resort.

## Chapter Thirteen

Briana spent the night at a budget motel, then drove the rest of the way to the resort. Heavy gray clouds hid the sun, threatening to dump snow any minute now. She'd rented a set of chains for the tires just in case. So far, she hadn't needed them.

Frigid air, crisp and sweet smelling, bit her cheeks as she got out of the car and looked around. Just the weekend, she promised herself. She needed time to pull herself together, to face the bitterness of loss.

A loss that rightfully hadn't been hers to begin with.

Depression weighed heavy in her chest as she lifted her overnight bag from the trunk. Something felt wrong. Pulling herself out of her self-pitying fog, she finally took conscious stock of her surroundings.

White smoke curled from the chimney, but the place appeared deserted. No cars packed the parking lot, no one traversed the restful landscape. The chairlifts heading up the mountainside hung motionless except for the gentle rocking created by intermittent gusts of pine-scented wind.

A resort that remained seventy-five-percent booked

year-round felt like a ghost town. True, the season hadn't officially started, but this was ridiculous...and eerie.

Come to think of it, she'd passed a couple of cars coming in the opposite direction, but hadn't encountered any traffic on the way up.

Her heart thumped in unease as fanciful thoughts crowded in—dumb scenarios like there'd been a mass evacuation and she was the only one who didn't know about it.

A high-pitched whine and a whooping noise had her head jerking around. She shaded her eyes and gripped her hair as the rotors of a lone helicopter whipped wind and bits of grass, then gently lifted off a cement pad.

So much for mass evacuation. The helicopter held only the pilot, no passengers. Which meant he'd probably dropped people off.

Hooking her bag over her shoulder, she went into the main lobby to register. A cozy fire crackled in the massive stone fireplace, yet nobody occupied the hunter-green-plaid couches and chairs grouped to invite conversation and relaxation after a strenuous day on the slopes.

Odd, she thought. The lodge was normally overrun with bodies, both day and night.

Okay, Briana reminded herself again before her mind took off on another tangent. There wasn't enough snow to stick to the ground, no reason for avid skiers to be hanging at the windows, praying for a fresh coat of powder.

After all, she hadn't brought skis, and had no plans

to exert herself other than taking long, healing walks through nature, far enough away from everyday life that she could find some balance.

Figuring the manager was in the back sipping hot chocolate or warmed brandy, Briana moved to the counter and placed her hand over the silver bell used universally by waiting customers to signal management.

It was then she got the uncanny feeling she was being watched. She curled her fingers into her palm, drew her hand back and slowly turned.

Joseph stood by the hearth, leaning against the mantel as if he'd been standing there for quite some time. But he hadn't. There hadn't been anyone in the room when she'd entered.

Her heart raced and for a minute she felt faint.

He looked tired and rumpled. His dark eyes had a weary cast, his jaw was stubbled with beard.

And he looked wonderful.

*Oh, Joseph,* she thought. *I have so many dreams to share. Please be there for me.* The words echoed so loudly in her mind, she wondered if she hadn't actually said them aloud. Dear Lord, she wanted to say them. But she had no right.

*She* was the one who couldn't be there for *him.*

"The snow has begun," he said softly.

She glanced out the window. Sometimes the sweetest heartache was the saddest fate. She'd run from him, yet he'd found her. And now, neither one would be going anywhere. The weather would prevent it. Mesmerized, she stared at the gentle but

steady mist of white that would soon slick the roads
and transform the pines into a glittery wonderland.

A wonderland where she would be trapped—at
least for a while. With Joseph.

Would she be able to be this close to him and keep
her secret?

"What happened, *querida?* What has caused your
sadness?"

Sighing, she put down her bag.

"Is it your memory? Have you remembered the
day?"

"No." The snow was now falling with a vengeance. Under the circumstances, it would be best to
head him off that subject. "Just baby hormones, I
guess."

"Smart baby, inspiring you to seek such a place of
romance."

*Romance.* Yes, the place inspired it with its cozy
fire and visions of cuddling under a down quilt. Then
again, Joseph, in any setting, would inspire romance.

She glanced around. "Speaking of the place, it appears deserted. I know the ski season isn't officially
open, but this is eerie."

He shrugged nonchalantly and Briana realized
something was up; she recognized the gesture. "Joseph...what did you do?"

"Rented a room."

"How many rooms?"

His brows lowered in defense, obviously expecting
opposition. "All of them."

And just that simply, laughter tickled her insides,
spilling over. "*All* of them?"

"Yes."

"And the ski lifts, too?"

"Those, too."

She shook her head, and tried to muffle the chuckle. "I should have known. You don't do anything if not in a grand style."

"You do not like my style?"

"It floors me, if you want to know the truth. However, I'm sure there are plenty of vacationers who are cursing your 'style' right about now. How in the world did you accomplish something like this?" She swept her hand in a gesture that encompassed the empty room.

"With a phone call."

That started her off on another bout of laughter. "A phone call? It would take months and a lot of money to empty out a place like this."

"Money, yes, but only a day."

"A day... You called *yesterday?* But you weren't here yesterday." His intended bride had been, though. And his brother—sent on a mission to pay her off. The memory turned her heart to lead.

"I got in last night." He still hadn't moved from his place by the mantel, and the intensity of his gaze was making her nervous.

"How did you find me? No, never mind. I can answer that myself. My cousin has a big mouth."

"Your cousin has a big heart."

"That, too." She cruised the room, touching the back of the sofa, a photograph of Tom Cruise holding a pair of skis, a bronze sculpture of a skier in racing form. Despite her outward air of nonchalance, her nerves were screaming. He was everything she wanted, everything she couldn't have.

But he was here.

"If I asked you to, would you stay here? In my arms?"

Her fingertips jerked, nearly knocking the sculpture over. "There's not much chance of leaving now, with the weather dumping ice on the roads."

"I think you know that is not what I'm asking." He pushed away from the mantel and moved slowly, intently toward her. "We have shared a room for the past few weeks, shared a bed, yet we have not shared the intimacy."

She couldn't look at him. Because if she did, she would agree to anything. "What we have is kind of like a vacation romance, Joseph. You'll be going home soon. I'll be staying here, or maybe even going back to the States. It's what we agreed on."

His tone was tight with the effort to control it. He stopped in front of her, nearly touching her. "I did not agree. And I wish to renegotiate."

The vulnerability in the softly spoken words snagged her attention, pierced her heart. She did look at him then, but found it impossible to look away. Would there be so much harm in it? One last memory? Dear heaven, she was like a drunk rationalizing just one more drink—and after that, just one more.

As though she were in the grip of addiction, words spilled out before guilt and willpower could call them back.

"Franco has a suite here. Crystal calls this his chalet, but he only owns one of the rooms—some-

times—more on a time share principle. I'm not sure
which room it is, but…'' He was so close she had
trouble drawing a breath. "The manager can tell
us—provided you didn't send him away, too?''

"He is still here. We have our choice of quarters,
any of them.'' His fingers toyed with the buttons on
the front of her coat. "I own the resort.''

"As of last night?''

"Yes.''

Another reminder of his power, of who he was.
"Can property transfer take place that fast?''

"There are still formalities to attend to. The cash
settlement, though, was more than enough to prove
good faith.''

"I can imagine.'' Actually, she couldn't imagine
anything except Joseph—his scent, his hands, his
heat. Dear Lord, she *wanted*. Wanted with an ache
that consumed her. Not the stinging ache of desire,
though. Something deeper. Much deeper.

"What about it, Briana?'' he asked softly. "You
did not answer my question.''

Question? His lips were so close, so enticing. She
replayed the conversation. "Renegotiate, you say?''

"I'd just as soon our relationship didn't hinge on
a bargaining table.'' His fingertips lightly stroked her
cheek.

She sighed. "I need those bargains, Joseph. I'd
thought to spend the weekend alone.'' She saw him
wince; saw the vulnerability, the frustration he banked
with gentleness.

"I can call the chopper back.''

The gentleness pushed her to the edge; that he gave

her a choice cinched her decision. "I might not be feeling quite so antisocial after all. I'd...I'd like to spend the weekend with you."

"At a distance?"

"No," she whispered.

He eased open the buttons on her coat, slipped warm palms around her hips. "Why only the weekend?"

"That's the best I can do, Joseph." Her shrug was meant to be brave; it ended up feeling sad and pitiful. The image of a bank draft flashed in her mind—a banknote with more zeros than the average person could count. "Take it or leave it."

"I'll take it. Just as I'll take you, any way I can get you." His mouth was warm and softer than she had thought possible. He didn't ask for explanations; just seemed to understand her struggle, accepted it. And with great care, he set about to ease the storm of uncertainty.

His fingers stroked soothingly over her face, then moved to the base of her neck as if he knew the tension that centered there. With the softest pressure, he took the kiss deeper, without fire or fury but with a seductive heat that was impossible to resist.

He drew back, looked deep into her eyes. "I do not want to lose you."

She placed her fingertips against his lips, unable to reassure him. Her throat ached, wouldn't allow any words past. With her eyes alone, she begged him. Begged him to give her a lifetime in one short night.

He took her hand, led her up a staircase and into

one of the rooms. Here, too, a fire crackled in a stone fireplace, casting a soft glow.

He closed the door, slipped the heavy coat from her shoulders, drew her head to his chest and just held her for long minutes. Warm, undemanding hands massaged her neck, easing away the tension in her shoulders.

Her emotions were too frayed to feel the hurried sting of desire. Instead, she just wanted to crawl inside him, to feel safe, loved; to pretend that there was plenty of time, that they could always be together.

Knowing they couldn't made her feel both urgent and hopeless.

Frigid wind pelted against the windowpanes, moaned through the chimney flue. With slow, deft hands, he undressed her, guiding her with care, drawing a quiet response that built like the first rays of morning sunlight, slowly, by increments, warmth growing with each notch of the ascent.

He roamed her face lightly with kisses, tenderly pressed his lips to her closed lids. And even when they were naked, he did nothing more than kiss her, hold her, running his hands over her back and shoulders, the sensitive spot at the base of her neck.

Joseph heard the subtle shift in her breathing, the faint quickening. He didn't know what had caused her flight here, didn't know what caused the terrible, hopeless sadness he saw in her clear green eyes, and he was terrified to push for answers.

Unable to put a name to the fear, he tried to ignore it, concentrated instead on Briana only. To give to her, all he had to give, hoping it would somehow be enough. He'd been so sure, so damned sure they were making headway.

He was learning, though, that with Briana, he couldn't be certain about anything. He could only hope and pray—and give. She tried to hide it, but there was a fragility about her tonight, a subtle air that told him she could very well shatter from something so innocent as a beam of moonlight. Her smile was strained, her laughter brittle yet brave. He'd gotten so used to her verve, her unflagging strength and spirit.

Yet tonight he needed to put aside those thoughts, to concentrate solely on her vulnerability.

So he kept his hands easy. The raised, mahogany bedposts creaked against coiled springs as he coaxed her down on the mattress padded with goose down. The fluffy cushion pillowed around them, molded to their bodies.

Firelight shivered over her skin where his hands roamed. Pressing his lips to her shoulder, the flare of her hips, the firm swell of her belly, he could smell the familiar trace of raspberries.

In the play of shadows dancing against the silk of her skin, he traced the faint blue veins in her swollen breasts, followed with gentle kisses, never lingering long in any one place. There were subtle changes in her body—changes he hadn't noted before. Her nipples pebbled, taunting him, yet he showered his attention on the whole of her, from the top of her head to her coral-tipped toes.

Her legs shifted restlessly beneath him, sliding

against the sheets, her breath now rushing between her parted lips.

Briana reached for him, realizing she'd been passive up to this point, taking without giving in return. Dazed, she watched as he kissed her palm, laid it back against the sheets.

"Joseph…"

"Let me," he whispered. "Just feel, *querida*."

And she did, letting her mind empty, lost in his touch, his scent, his tender ministrations. He filled her senses and left no room for outside intrusions. Just touch and taste and heat, a heat that built and burned and exploded.

Her breath trembled at the pleasure, the comfort, the love. And when at last he eased their bodies together as one, the exquisite, utterly focused tenderness made her weep.

JOSEPH TOSSED ANOTHER log on the fire, and watched her sleep. He frowned when her movements became restless, as if she were held in the grip of a nightmare.

Easing a hip down beside her on the mattress, he kissed her brow and smoothed her bangs back off her forehead.

Her green eyes snapped open, her chest heaving on a startled breath.

"Bad dream?"

She stared at him for several minutes. Eyes dazed from sleep and restless dreams cleared, and flashed with an emotion he couldn't identify. All he knew was that it had his gut twisting into knots.

He'd always been a man to face his problems head-on. In this instance, with Briana, he realized he was little more than a coward. Her words echoed in his mind. *Only the weekend. That's the best I can do.* He'd said he would take what she could give. He knew he wanted more.

She's the only one for me, he thought. No, he amended. *They* were the ones. Briana and the baby. He could not bear to lose them.

Dismissing the panic, he patted her hip. "Hungry?"

"Yes." Her eyes widened. "No!" Scurrying from beneath the covers, she made a mad dash for the bathroom.

"Ah, *querida*," he said, following her, trying to soothe, yet feeling inept in light of her misery. "I would take this sickness upon myself if I could."

She swatted at his hand, pushed him aside. "Go away. At least leave me with a little dignity."

He ignored her grumbling and pressed a cool cloth to her forehead. Her skin was pale, making the sprinkling of freckles across her nose stand out prominently. When the worst of the bout was over, she sat back on the cold tiles of the bathroom floor and looked up at him.

"Pregnancy shouldn't be this miserable. Why is that, do you suppose?"

"I think it has something to do with Eve taking a bite of the apple."

"Well, Adam ate it, too," she griped. "How come guys don't have to go through this?"

"Ah, but we do," he said softly. "I do. Each time you feel pain, sickness...sadness, I feel it, too."

Her eyes filled with tears. He was better than any fantasy man she could have dreamed up. Impatiently, she brushed away the moisture, did a mental check to see how she felt. Hungry, she decided, amazed. To go from violently ill to ravenous in a matter of minutes seemed ridiculous. But there it was.

She looked back up at him, determined not to let his gentle words derail her. "While you were busy tossing your money around and giving the staff a surprise vacation, did you by chance plan for meals?"

"The kitchen is stocked, I am told."

"You're slipping, Prince. You should have kept the cook. I'm only mediocre at best, and I'd wager you haven't got a clue."

"You could not be mediocre if you tried."

Oh, he always said the sweetest things. She held out a hand and let him help her to her feet, allowing herself another moment just to lean against him, to absorb his heat, to regain her balance.

Steady now, she drew back, snagged a thick terry robe from a hook on the door and pushed her arms into the sleeves.

"Let's go raid the fridge."

The fire had burned down in the main room. While Joseph built it back up, Briana searched the cupboards of the enormous kitchen. She found a gigantic box of blueberry muffin mix and did a mental calculation of measures. The mix was designed to feed thirty.

Next she selected eggs, bacon, butter and cheese from the refrigerator, set them on the counter and searched the overhead racks for the right-size pan.

Joseph wandered in, raised a brow. "I guess you *are* hungry."

"I think I forgot to eat last night." Pain stung her chest. The reason she hadn't eaten was because Joseph had been making such tender love to her. It was an experience that had exhausted her already overwrought emotions, sending her into a restless sleep filled with dreams of babies dressed as royalty, standing outside palace gates, peering in.

Not good enough to live within.

She touched a hand to her stomach, made a silent vow to her child, and promised that she would always protect it, that she would never put this sweet baby in a position where someone might find him lacking.

And a royal baby, no matter which side of the blanket he was conceived on, shouldn't be found lacking....

Unless its mother had less-than-perfect lineage—which she did, in the eyes of royalty.

Muffin batter splattered over the side of the bowl and the wooden spoon nearly snapped in two under the force she unconsciously applied. Making an effort to swallow her agitation and hopelessness, she stared at the bruised blueberries and the mixture that was now a deep purple.

She felt a scream building, knew her leaky eyes were about to spout. Exasperated all over again, she divided the batter into six tins and placed the tray in the oven. Purple muffins were proof she was no great shakes in the kitchen.

From the corner of her eye, she kept tabs on Joseph who prowled around the room, pressing buttons and playing with the appliances. Suddenly, the beaters of a heavy-duty stand mixer clattered explosively against an aluminum bowl.

Briana jumped as if she'd been shot. "Would you cut that out?"

Reluctantly, he halted the spinning bowl, hit the power button, studied it further as if it were the most fascinating thing.

"Haven't you ever seen kitchen gadgets?" she asked, clutching at her bossom, which heaved under the terry robe.

"I am rarely in the kitchen."

"That answers my next question. You can't cook a lick, can you?"

"I am best at ordering in."

"Figures. So much for the sharing thing."

He stepped behind her and slid his arms around her waist. "I can learn."

She swallowed an absurd giggle. "To feel morning sickness?"

"Yes. And to cook."

"I can't teach you the one, but you can get started on the other." She slipped from his arms, took eggs out of the carton, started to hand them to him. "On second thought, you'd better just sit down and let me do it. I object to eggshells in my omelets."

"You wound me, *querida*." He took the egg from her hand, cracked it against the side of a bowl and emptied the contents without adding a single piece of shell.

"I'm impressed."

"Nothing to it. I saw the procedure demonstrated

once while I was flipping channels on the television.''
He continued to crack eggs until Briana laughed and
placed a hand on his arm.

"I think that'll do it. We're not feeding an army.''

The sweet smell of muffins wafted from the oven,
making her mouth water. The bacon, however, gave
her pause. It wouldn't take much to send her racing
back to the bathroom.

"I think we'll skip the bacon," she said. "Unless
you're one of those guys who has to have meat with
every meal?''

"I am rather partial to that menu choice, but not
inflexible. Eggs and muffins will do fine.''

"I like an agreeable man." Wait till he saw the
color of the muffins.

"See? More things in common. Soon we will be
thinking alike.''

"I doubt it. Sit.''

"Excellent, Briana. You are a natural at giving orders. A fine talent for a princess to possess.''

She pointed to a chair, refusing to be drawn into
his commonality game. They might be worlds apart
in social class, but their hearts were a tight fit.

Too tight.

In no time, she set steaming omelets and fragrant,
*purple* muffins before them, as well as coffee, tea and
juice. Joseph didn't even blink at the strange-looking
breakfast rolls. He rose and retrieved a carton of milk
from the refrigerator and placed it in front of Briana.

She wrinkled her nose. "I draw the line at milk.''

"The baby needs milk.''

"How do you know? More channel surfing?''

"No. But I would think it does." He didn't sound so sure.

"It'll get its quota from the calcium in the vitamins I'm taking."

"Are you sure?" His hand hovered over the carton.

"You want to see me run for the bathroom again?"

"Do not tease. It upsets me to see you ill."

"It upsets me even more." She buttered a muffin, and took a bite. "Looks like a Smurf, but it doesn't taste half bad."

"What is a Smurf?"

"Little blue people? Cartoon-like characters?" At his blank look, she shrugged. "So, what kind of prince business did you have to do?" That, too, brought a blank look. "The trip," she clarified.

"Ah." He took an unusual amount of time and care buttering his own muffin. "A doctor friend received a patent on a procedure that has been experimental up to this point. I flew to the States to show support."

"The States? In two days?"

"The Concorde is a fine invention."

"You flew in the Concorde? You lucky duck."

"You wish to ride in the aircraft? I will take you."

"There you go, tossing your money around again." Figuratively. "Bribery is an ugly trait."

"But effective?"

"For the weak of character. Which I'm not." At least, she hadn't been. Before Joseph.

All she needed to do was close her eyes to see dreams of tomorrow. Vivid dreams with Joseph by her side. And their child. He promised her undying love, companionship, and as much travel as she could stand—the very thing she'd longed for since childhood. Yet she couldn't accept it, knew that even if she did, if they tried to make a go of it, the relationship would sour. Joseph had responsibilities, and she and the child growing in her womb didn't fit into the picture.

She placed her palm over her abdomen, wishing she could share her news with him, knowing the secret would remain locked in her heart.

Thank God, her thoughts weren't drifting through the air. If he could see them, hear them, she would be lost.

The omelet before her suddenly became unappetizing. She pushed it away, girding herself for what she knew would be the performance of her life.

"I met your betrothed," she said brightly.

Joseph frowned. "Who?"

"Don't tell me you've forgotten her. Raquel?"

"I told you, I am not marrying her."

"According to your father and hers, you are. Antonio even agrees."

"Antonio?" A muscle ticked in his jaw. "What is going on, Briana?"

"Raquel and Antonio came by the flower shop looking for you. Mr. Santiago insisted, I think, figuring you and his daughter could patch up your differences. I told them you were out of town. I assumed they'd wait on your boat."

"No. They didn't. Are you certain it was Raquel with Tony?"

"Stunning woman? Incredibly long hair? Dynamite body?"

"I wouldn't know. I have never seen her hair down."

"You're missing a treat. So when are you leaving?"

"When you are ready."

She smiled even though her heart was breaking. It was the hardest thing she'd ever done in her life. "You know I can't go."

Joseph carefully laid down the fork that bent in his hand. Panic gripped him, turning his blood to ice. "Why are you so set on sending me into the arms of another woman?"

"Because that's where you belong."

That he couldn't read her emotions made him feel all the more ungrounded. "No. It is not. Marrying Raquel is a fate that is no longer acceptable to me. Especially now that I've had a taste of what true love is. I set out to choose my own queen, Briana. For love. And I've found that in you, a woman who yells at me and treats me like a real person instead of a prince. You make me laugh, keep me on my toes."

A woman who was pregnant and—crazy as it seemed—had no memory of how she got that way. But he didn't care.

She scooted her chair back and rose. "Just because I yell at you doesn't recommend me as a lifetime mate. In fact, it should do just the opposite. Excuse me."

Before he could stop her, she left the room. Joseph didn't immediately go after her. He needed a moment to find some equilibrium.

She was slipping away from him and he felt helpless to stop her. He'd run circles around the sun chasing after her and he didn't know what else was left to try. He was fighting for his life, here, and needed to be prepared.

SHE WAS DRESSED AND had her bags packed by the time he came upstairs.

"The snowplows'll have the roads cleared by now," she said with false brightness.

"Don't do this, Briana."

"Do what?" She deliberately misunderstood. "Leave? I've got a job waiting. I can't take the chance of another snowstorm. You came in a helicopter, right? I suppose I could give you a ride if you want."

"The chopper can take both of us."

"Are you kidding? Once I got behind the wheel of that Mercedes I was hooked." *No, I wasn't. All I could think about was you. Your strong hands gripping the steering wheel, the smell of your cologne mingling with the leather seats.* She hooked the latch on her suitcase, faced him with squared shoulders and a stiff smile. She intended to leave the car at the marina—by his boat, which would soon be departing.

"What must I do to convince you? I love you, Briana. I love that child growing inside you. I do not care about your lost memory or what you might have done on that day or any other day. After all we have shared, can you honestly tell me you do not feel the way I feel?"

"I don't know that I have the right to feel *any* way about you."

"I am giving you the right."

Oh, it hurt. Hurt to look at him. To lie. To replay the memories—to know they couldn't be. She wasn't the woman for him. She had to let him go. Had to convince him to *let* her let him go.

It was like slashing a piece of flesh, in one sharp and stinging stroke, inflicting a wound that might never heal. But she must.

She reached for his hand, placed the necklace there, curled his fingers around the stones and tortured herself for another moment by simply holding on. Her insides felt as if they were tearing apart, ripping one bloody seam at a time. The ache in her throat was nearly intolerable. It moved to her ears, pressing in.

*Please go,* she begged silently. *Before I cave in.* Or fall apart. Before she said to hell with it and selfishly took something for herself—at the expense of Joseph's kingdom. His way of life.

"Someday, when you're king, you'll realize I was right."

"What about in the meantime?"

"Raquel can make you happy if you give her a chance. She's a good woman, Joseph."

He swore, in Spanish, English and German. "I will renounce my title."

She touched her fingertips to his lips. "Don't."

"You hold my heart and soul, Briana."

"I don't deserve it. It'll never work between us."

"I will *make* it work. Do you not love me?"

"Not enough." She saw him wince and nearly lost her nerve. Oh, she did love him, heart and soul. But love wouldn't move mountains or change the traditions of an entire country. "I got caught up in the fairy tale. You offered me a way out in grand style. But I can't take that, Joseph. I can't allow somebody else to fix my problems."

"Tell me what I have to do and I'll do it. I've given everything I have, I don't know what else to try." Desperation tinged his voice, a desperation no prince should either display or feel. "How do I make you see that I'm going out of my mind, Briana? I have no pride. Name your price."

"Joseph, please. It's out of our hands. It has been since the day each of us was born—you to royalty, me in a county hospital in Ohio. You think that makes no difference, but it does. I'd shrivel up to nothing if I had to watch you day in and day out, fighting my battles, fighting your family and your country for my acceptance."

"Bri—"

She shook her head, didn't even bother to stop the tears that slid down her cheeks. "I can't," she whispered. "I don't— It's over, Joseph. Please, go home."

# Chapter Fourteen

The look on his face as she'd left the resort haunted her for weeks. Morning sickness coupled with stress nearly incapacitated her, yet she kept busy. The bathrooms gleamed, the curtains had been jerked down and laundered, not a single weed dared show its spiky head in her garden. Marie's Flower Shop was so organized, Marie had finally shooed Briana home with laughing exasperation, claiming she couldn't find a blessed thing now that all the supplies had cataloged spaces and cubby holes.

And still, Briana couldn't get Joseph out of her mind, couldn't get past the sadness of having to let him go. She told herself he would be fine. Once back in his own country, he would forget all about her, marry the beautiful, acceptable Raquel and make even more beautiful, more acceptable babies.

Her heart gave a painful squeeze. She stood in the middle of the front room, looked around frantically for something to do, something to beat back the terrible scream that threatened. If she could just keep busy, she could outrun it.

She was about to attack the phantom dust on the

already sparkling picture frames when Crystal breezed in, Peppe in her arms.

"Still moping, I see."

"I'm not moping. I'm doing some much-needed spring cleaning." The scream receded like a ghost, slyly waiting for darkness and loneliness to return, waiting for a better opportunity to torment.

"It is not spring. Snap out of it, Briana."

Peppe barked to punctuate the admonishment.

Tears filled Briana's eyes. She couldn't seem to stop them lately. It was disgusting. She sank onto the sofa, gulped air to hold the madness at bay.

"Oh, Bri, go to him. Tell him you made a mistake."

"I didn't make a mistake." She picked up a red throw pillow, hugged it to her stomach. "He's better off without me. I'd ruin his life."

"That is not possible. I do not believe I have ever seen a man look at a woman the way your Joseph looks at you."

"Looked," Briana corrected. "And he's not *my* Joseph."

Crystal ignored her. "I have never seen a man touch a woman so tenderly, with only his eyes. And I find that I am horribly jealous and must speak to Franco about his own attentiveness."

Did Joseph really look at her that way? "You were just seeing things."

"If you believe that, then you are as blind as Peppe." The little dog barked at hearing his name. "Do you not realize you and I are holding back, using the same excuses?"

"I don't see how you can compare me to you and Franco. Your future is paved with perfectness."

"Now that I am assured of a child," Crystal agreed. "Franco wanted to marry me regardless of children. I am the one who wanted to orchestrate his future, the one who refused marriage unless it could be according to my terms and conditions. I worried over not being good enough—as you do. Yet love is blind to flaws, Bri. We must close our eyes and press forward. Trust, as Peppe does."

"You can't compare my life to a dog's."

"Why not? He has a lot more gumption than you or I. He is independent and ornery, yet smart enough to trust that we will be there for him if he loses his way. Just as I must trust that Franco will be there for me, flaws and all. As your Joseph wishes to be there for you. It does not matter to him that your lineage is that of a stray mutt."

The sound of a woman clearing her throat at the open doorway had Briana turning with a start.

"I fear I must object to the future royal princess of Valldoria being referred to as a mutt."

JOSEPH HAD BECOME a mere shell of himself, but he couldn't find the energy to care. Everyone worried about him, he knew—from the household maids—who'd received a substantial raise—to the citizens of Valldoria who sent mail and inquired daily. Speculation was rampant over the crown prince who'd had his heart broken.

Added to his own turmoil, there was dissension between King Marcos and Queen Isabel. Surprisingly, the queen had packed an army of trunks and left.

An epidemic, it appeared. All the women had caught the same bug. Now Raquel was missing.

And it was their wedding day.

Briana was gone from his life, the heiress had flown the coop and his mother was off to who-knew-where. So why was he sitting on a wooden boat dock on the palace grounds dressed in a crisply pressed black-and-platinum uniform, a crown prince's equivalent of a tuxedo?

There was a full-scale search for Raquel who'd disappeared without a trace. His wedding day appeared doomed, which wasn't a news flash. In his heart, the day had signaled doom anyway.

The chapel was decorated, the flowers already wilting, tapers burning to wax puddles. He should be worried over the whereabouts of his bride, or at least have a care about the possibility of the church burning down due to unattended candles.

He couldn't find an ounce of emotion. He was dead inside, felt a misery that went bone deep. The days kept moving faster, but the nights were an eternity. Silence stalked his waking hours, filled with memories of Briana, her touch, her scent. In his mind, he could see her, feel her, but all the warmth had died. What good were memories when they only left him cold—frozen inside, his heart chained in misery?

The wood slats of the dock creaked as his brother eased down beside him, yet Joseph never took his eyes off the serene surface of the lake.

For several minutes, the two sat in silence. Stately

oaks cast tall shadows across the expanse of water and the gentle trickling sound of a waterfall in the distance twisted Joseph's gut, reminding him of Briana, of another waterfall in a beautiful grotto that housed bizarre rocks.

"I am beginning to wonder at this pattern we appear to have developed regarding important ceremonies and certain princesses-to-be," Antonio said jovially. "I have once again been dispatched to hasten you along."

Joseph remained silent, skipped a stone over the surface of the lake, marring its serenity with circular ripples. Unable to resist the competition, Antonio joined the sport, his own rock skipping twice more than Joseph's. When he didn't gloat over the triumph, Joseph turned to face him.

"The bride has been found?"

"That is the word."

Joseph couldn't even find the interest to ask where Raquel had flitted off to, even though it was totally out of character for the heiress.

He sighed, tossed another stone that landed with a plunk in the water. "I will show up, Tony. Do not worry. I know my duty."

And in understanding his duty, he also realized he'd been asking Briana to be somebody he, himself, had found intolerable. He'd been asking her to live through him, under his protection—offering to smooth the way in his country, by royal command if need be. And in doing so, he would be asking her to give up a part of herself—her spontaneity, her laughter and independence, her easy acceptance of herself.

Worry over the child she carried not being his—her guilt over that knowledge—would suck the life out of her.

And he couldn't do it, was forced to respect her wishes even though it caused a rent in his heart he doubted would ever heal. He would not put that vibrant woman in a position of living her life through him, under the dictates of his title and centuries of tradition, amid the imagined censure of the king and queen and his countrymen.

Still, realization and understanding didn't make acceptance any easier. He couldn't bear the thought of her having that child alone; wanted to be there to hold her if her memory came back, just in case it was a bad memory. She might need a pair of arms to hold her close. *Dios,* he wanted those arms to be his.

Antonio sent another rock sailing. "I can understand if you are annoyed with me and prefer I not stand in as your best man."

Joseph didn't feel annoyed, he just felt numb. "We are brothers, Tony, regardless. I know you were only following orders when you went to see Briana. And you are still my choice."

"But Raquel Santiago is not."

"I will uphold my duty," he repeated by rote, his jaw aching with the force of his clenched teeth. Odd how he could be numb and still experience pain, still bleed, feel as if life were yawning before him in a deep chasm of loneliness.

"Perhaps you will find that duty is not so intolerable, after all."

Briana had said similar words to him. Didn't everybody know he was losing it, here? Didn't they realize that there was a very real possibility he could not survive without Briana in his life? He looked at his brother, frowned at the sly grin on Antonio's handsome devil-may-care features. He, too, was dressed in Valldorian ceremonial garb.

"What I find intolerable is that you have never experienced the excruciating pain of love."

"Bite your tongue, Your Highness! I am allergic to love."

Joseph shook his head, and gave a rough chuckle. "Someday you'll fall, Tony. And when you do, I hope I'm there to see it." He rose, extending his hand to his brother. "Let's go."

The clock tower to the east of the palace chimed the hour, but Joseph didn't concern himself over his tardiness. After all, the disappearing bride had caused the delay.

Two dynasties would unite today and for the life of him, Joseph just couldn't see the point. The size of the opulent palace itself was testament to his family's riches. He didn't need an heiress to add to his net worth. He had more money than ten people—a *hundred* people—could spend in a lifetime.

He needed love.

The chapel on the palace grounds was filled to overflowing. Beyond the gates were silken ropes to hold back the cheering crowd as a black limousine flying Valldorian flags wound its way up the drive.

Joseph and Antonio entered through the side doors, and took their place at the front of the church.

"Pretty good turnout," Antonio commented.

Nodding automatically, Joseph kept his gaze on the platinum candelabra. So, the wax hadn't melted after all. Someone had extinguished them before they'd been reduced to puddles. All the wicks were black, except one. The center one. The one the bride and groom would light together in the ceremonial tradition that signified uniting their lives and hearts as one.

His heart felt like a stone in his chest. How the hell could he pledge everlasting love to anyone besides Briana?

"In case you are interested," Antonio said, "I have the ring."

Again, Joseph's nod was automatic.

Organ music swelled. Expected to turn, Joseph did so, focusing his gaze on an uncanny ray of light that beamed through the arched stained-glass windows, landing right on the bride who stood at the open double doors, volumes of netting covering her face.

Typical, he thought. He'd rarely seen Raquel without some sort of elaborate headdress. *Por Dios,* she was likely to scare the hell out of him when he came upon her in the marriage bed. It would be as though a stranger had invaded his bedroom. A stranger who did not have a smile that could rival the sun, or an improper laugh that would brighten even the staunchest grouch.

The bride, her white dress trailing a six-foot-long train, came up the endless aisle alone. Odd that Santiago wasn't escorting his daughter. Then again, Joseph hadn't involved himself in these wedding preparations, hadn't attended any rehearsals or even spoken to his intended.

He'd left those details up to the women of the families—his mother and hers. Amazing in itself that the fete was even going on, what with both Raquel and his mother vanishing at the last minute.

But money spoke, he knew. With enough palms greased, even an elaborate affair such as this could be pulled off in a day's time and still give the appearance that preparations had taken an eternity.

An eternity.

*Dios.* Could he do it?

The bride drew level with him. Altar boys had relit the candles—all but the center one. The priest, robed and sashed, stood before them with an open Bible.

"Joseph Lorenzo Castillo, crown prince of Valldoria," the priest began. "Do you come here of your own free will, and do you take this woman to be your future queen?"

He smelled raspberries. He closed his eyes, his gut twisting in panic. He had to get out of here. Had to find her, make her understand that he couldn't survive without her.

Antonio nudged him. The bride turned, her stiff lace brushing against Joseph's chest, nearly knocking him off balance.

"Your Highness?" the priest prompted.

He couldn't do it. Joseph shook his head. "I don't—"

"By heaven, you'd better!"

Stunned, Joseph watched as the bride snatched at the veil, batting at the netting as if she were swatting at a swarm of angry bees. It took several tries to shove it away from her face.

A face that haunted his dreams.

The scent of raspberries swirled around him.

"Briana…?"

Laughing green eyes met his. For a minute he thought he was going to embarrass himself and blow his princely image by fainting. He reached for her, carefully touched shaking fingertips to her soft cheek, afraid she was a mere figment of his imagination. Her hand cupped his, her sensual lips pressing against the center of his palm.

"How…?" He couldn't seem to complete a sentence.

"I heard you were missing a bride and I thought I'd stand in."

The priest cleared his throat. "I fear I am losing control and must hurry before there is a breach of epic proportions right here in the house of God." His voice rose. "Who gives this woman in marriage?"

"Her mother and I do."

Joseph's head whipped around. Thomas Duvaulle, resplendent in a black tuxedo, rolled his wheelchair up the center aisle, flanked on one side by Briana's mother and on the other by King Marcos and Queen Isabel. Behind them were her two sisters, her brother, Crystal and a man he assumed was Franco.

Briana smiled gently and waved, causing the crowd to chuckle and shift and sigh. Everything within him softened and fell into place. All was as it should be. This woman charmed him as no other could.

She looked back at him. "Your mother came and got me. She's a very persuasive woman. And a maniac, if you want to know the truth."

Joseph's eyebrow rose at this last description of the queen. His Briana was going to shake up the palace but good. "A maniac, you say?"

She grinned. "I mean that in the most complimentary way."

"Of course."

"In no time at all, she whipped everybody into shape, and sent frequent-flyer miles soaring with the way she flew people in and out of countries around the world—flowers, dress designers...my parents." She paused for breath, pinning him with a look that held the barest hint of panic.

A panic that he found charming and not at all threatening.

"You didn't answer the question," she said.

"The question?"

"Will you take me?"

"Ah, *querida*, absolutely. With my heart and soul and everything else I have to give."

Briana's eyes filled with tears. She was terrified by this whirlwind wedding, by the mass of people, by the life-style she was about to embrace. But Joseph eased her fears, made her feel strong, invincible, loved beyond all doubt.

"You always say the sweetest things. And give the most priceless gifts." Together they could see the world, just as she'd promised her father. And with the surgery Joseph had made possible, her father could join them.

"Dad told me you wanted him to walk me down the aisle. In the interests of expediency since I'm car-

rying the royal baby in my womb, would you settle
for him walking at our child's christening?''

''I will settle for anything if it involves you. And
I am glad that you have accepted that this child will
be royalty.'' He placed his palm at her stomach.

''You'd better believe *she'll* be royalty. I still have
no memory of that one day, but as it turns out, mine
and Crystal's tests were mixed up. She and Franco
are expecting in five months. Our baby needs to cook
for another seven.''

''Seven? But...?'' Awe turned his eyes liquid,
turned the caress of his palm against her stomach incredibly reverent as he searched her features for con-
firmation.

''I'm carrying *your* baby, Joseph. That first night...
You remember, don't you?''

His dark eyes ignited with a fire that surely wasn't
appropriate in a church. ''I will never forget,
*querida.*''

The priest lowered his Bible and looked with un-
holy interest from bride to groom and back again like
an avid spectator at a tennis match.

King Marcos, who was obviously still getting used
to the idea of breaking centuries of strict and correct
tradition, felt it was in his best interests to restore a
modicum of control.

He stood, causing the whole congregation to scram-
ble to their feet. With exasperated amusement, he
waved them back to their seats.

''Son, could you save the chitchat with your bride
for later? I, for one, am looking forward to a 'wedding
night' with my own queen, who has been giving me

the cold shoulder since I tried to make my son put duty before love.'' He glanced fondly at his wife, who smiled and linked her fingers with his.

The crowd murmured respectfully, yet the bride and groom ignored him and simply gazed into each other's eyes, desire arcing at the mention of wedding nights.

Exhaling a resigned breath, King Marcos sat back down. ''I wonder if they realize there's a microphone up there broadcasting their royal secrets,'' he grumbled.

''Hush,'' Isabel admonished. ''Our people were convinced Joseph was a preemie. We will report the same with the next generation of royalty.''

King Marcos rolled his eyes. ''The proverbial cat's already out of the bag.'' But his queen hushed him again, not wanting to miss a word of the royal exchange taking place in such an unconventional manner.

''You lied, *querida*,'' Joseph said softly. ''You *do* love me.''

''Don't be ridiculous,'' she whispered. ''I'm just after your money.''

''And the title?''

Her shoulders lifted. ''I could get used to it. Princess Bri,'' she said, trying it out.

''I like the sound of that.''

She gazed at him, feeling her heart swell with such happiness she thought she would burst. ''I love you, Prince Joseph.''

There was that look again, she thought dimly, the one Crystal had likened to a caress. With his eyes only, he held her—gently, reverently, with a love so powerful it touched. Everyone in the church must have felt it, too. Collective sighs swept the enormous chapel.

"And I love you, Princess Briana."

His head lowered, his lips touched hers, warm and filled with promise, a promise of endless nights of passion and a lifetime of happiness. It was a kiss that contained all the love and longing in his heart. A love and longing that matched her own.

The priest cleared his throat—again. He'd done it so many times in the past few minutes he was in danger of developing an inflammation. "Technically—if anybody is in the least interested—I feel honor-bound to point out that the bride is not *yet* a princess."

He could have saved his breath.

Joseph's hands framed Briana's face, his fingers unhinging two of the pins that held her hair beneath the veil. He angled her head, pressing their bodies closer, his legs lost in the voluminous satin gown. The world receded, leaving just the two of them, hearts speaking, lips clinging, sealing vows not yet spoken.

"I am an old man with bad knees," the priest muttered. "Antonio, clearly you must uphold your duties as best man and endeavor to restore ceremonial protocol."

Antonio grinned and tapped Joseph on the shoulder. When he got no response, he shrugged and gave a delighted laugh.

"Go for it, Prince."

In years to come, it would be touted as the most unusual, most romantic wedding in history.

# He's every woman's fantasy, but only one woman's dream come true.

For the first time Harlequin American Romance brings you THE ULTIMATE...in romance, pursuit and seduction—our most sumptuous series ever. Because wealth, looks and a bod are nothing without that one special woman.

# THE ULTIMATE...

## Pursuit

*They're*
#711 ~~SHE'S~~ THE ONE! by Mindy Neff
January 1998

## Stud

#715 HOUSE HUSBAND by Linda Cajio
February 1998

## Seduction

#723 HER PRINCE CHARMING by Nikki Rivers
April 1998

## Catch

#729 MASQUERADE by Mary Anne Wilson
June 1998

HARLEQUIN®

AMERICAN ◆ ROMANCE®

## HOW TO MARRY...

# A Real-Live Sheikh

You loved the original
"How To Marry..." trilogy so much
that we're bringing you more of
the fun and excitement of
husband hunting!

Join Jacqueline Diamond
for some all-important pointers on
how to catch this sultry, sexy
daddy who happens to be a
real-live sheikh!

Don't miss #716 **A REAL-LIVE SHEIKH**
in February 1998. Watch for more
"How To Marry..." titles coming
in the months ahead!

Available wherever Harlequin books
are sold.

# Prepare yourself for the
# Harlequin American Romance
# Blizzard of 1998!

**Question:**

What happens when a runaway bride, a young mother and a schoolteacher on a field trip with seven little girls get stranded in a blizzard?

**Answer:**

Not to worry, they'll each have a hot-blooded man to wrap them in sizzling male heat till the thaw—and forever after!

This winter cozy up with **Cathy Gillen Thacker's** new trilogy of romantic comedies for a case of cabin fever you'll never want to cure.

BRIDES, BABIES & Blizzards

**Snowbound Bride (#713)**
February 1998

**Hot Chocolate Honeymoon (#717)**
March 1998

**Snow Baby (#721)**
April 1998

Available wherever Harlequin books are sold.

**Look for these titles—**
**available at your favorite retail outlet!**

**BORN IN THE USA: Love, marriage—**
**and the pursuit of family!**

Look us up on-line at: http://www.romance.net

BUSA4